PLAN OF STONEHENGE

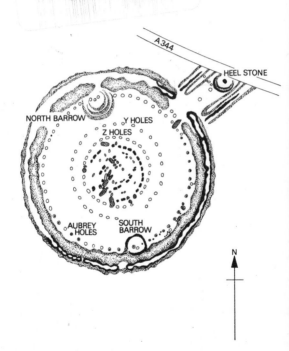

Hole
...tion
...tone
...... Stone standing
...... Stone fallen

A 344

HEEL STONE

NORTH BARROW

Y HOLES

Z HOLES

AUBREY HOLES

SOUTH BARROW

N

Scale 0   50   100 ft
         30 m

The Observer's Book of

ANCIENT AND ROMAN BRITAIN

HAROLD PRIESTLEY

WITH 74 BLACK AND WHITE PHOTOGRAPHS
10 PAGES OF MAPS AND 4 LINE DRAWINGS

FREDERICK WARNE & CO LTD
FREDERICK WARNE & CO INC
LONDON · NEW YORK

ACKNOWLEDGEMENTS

The author and publishers wish to thank the following for their kind permission to reproduce photographs used in this book: Aerofilms Ltd for photos on pages 13 (below), 43, 68, 76, 77, 78, 112, 113, 121, 125, 143, 152, 159, 170, 171 and 175; J. Allan Cash Ltd for photos on pages 28, 31 (below), 82 and 139; Barnaby's Picture Library for photos on pages 33 (photographer Richard Gee), 41 (photographer Harold Jones), 49 and 105 (photographer P. Loud), 124 (photographer William F. Meadows), 64 and 65 (photographer Don Williams); Janet and Colin Bord for photos on pages 6 (above), 13 (above), 52, 73, 74, 85, 88, 93, 95, 96, 97, 99, 100, 116, 119, 120, 123, 126, 130, 133 (above), 135, 136, 168, 174 and 176; The British Tourist Authority for photos on pages 6 (below), 31 (above), 55, 59, 148 and 161; Will Green for photos on pages 40 and 70; Eric Kay for photos on pages 50, 61, 71, 109, 133, 144, 155 and 167; Ministry of Works (Crown copyright reserved) for photo on page 164; and Scottish Tourist Board for photo on page 81.

The author also gives his grateful thanks to the Newham Library Service for help in obtaining catalogues, pamphlets etc.

Library of Congress Catalog
Card No. 74-21042

ISBN 0 7232 1544 8

Filmset by BAS Printers Limited, Wallop, Hampshire
Printed in Great Britain by Morrison & Gibb Ltd,
London and Edinburgh

CONTENTS

A general view of Silbury Hill Wiltshire

Roman Wall at Housteads Northumberland

HOW TO USE THIS BOOK

Ancient and Roman Britain lists and describes what may be seen at some of the thousands of sites which exist in Great Britain today. It will be of value to the amateur who wishes to learn something of the ancient history of our country in a practical way.

It covers all the area in Britain that came under Roman influence, both north and south of the two Roman walls and includes Dumfries and Galloway, Borders, Lothian, Central Scotland, Fife and much of Tayside. It excludes from the main text Strathclyde, Grampian, Highlands, Western Isles, Orkney and Shetland but makes mention of the most important sites in these regions in a special short appendix.

The Gazetteer, which forms the greater part of the book, concentrates on sites which in general are most accessible, unique or visually rewarding. Among these are many that are less known but are worth a visit. Most are within reach either by car, train or other forms of public transport, but since prehistoric peoples had a special affinity for heath and moorland, the search for causewayed camps, stone circles, barrows and hill-forts gives plenty of scope for the younger and more athletic.

The sites are listed in alphabetical order, though in addition the Gazetteer contains the following group entries: **brochs** (Scotland), **caves and rock shelters, mines, quarries and industrial sites, Roman barrows, forts and signal stations, forts of the Saxon Shore, frontier works, legionary fortresses, roads, towns** and **villas.** The section on frontier works includes military establishments between the two Roman walls and, north of these, to the limits of Roman penetration. Works south of

Hadrian's Wall are covered under other headings. For reasons of space sites under state guardianship are marked **DE** (Department of the Environment) and those under the National Trust are marked **NT**.

Since also some parts of Great Britain may contain many important sites within a very few square miles, it has been found advisable to make a few local groups either under the heading of a locality or of a special feature that dominates it. These groups are **Anglesey, the Antonine Wall, Avebury and neighbouring sites, the Bristol Iron Age hill-forts, Cornwall (West , Crosby village settlements, Cumbria; the Dorset Cursus and neighbouring sites, Hadrian's Wall, Rothbury cairns and hill-forts, Northumberland; Stonehenge and its neighbourhood, Wooler (Northumberland) and district.**

The Gazetteer does not claim to be comprehensive, for with such a wealth of remains still in existence, a whole library of reference books would be needed to cover them all. Lack of space has not permitted the description of the many relics, grave-goods etc. yielded by excavation, but these may be seen at public and private museums either on the sites or in the county towns.

Since the recent local government reforms, boundaries have been changed and new authorities created. Westmorland and Cumberland have become Cumbria, new counties have been carved out around Bristol (Avon), Liverpool (Merseyside), Newcastle (Tyne and Wear) and Greater Manchester. New names too have appeared in Wales and Scotland which may at first be strange to the explorer. Since also the metric system is being adopted in Britain, metric units of weights, measures, area etc. are interposed in brackets after the old British units.

It is hoped that this book will serve as an introduction which will lead the explorer into further excursions in the study of ancient history and archaeology.

KEY POINTS

The maps provide a number of Key Points which are an important feature of the book. These Key Points have been located at places from which a visitor may without too much difficulty visit a certain number of sites, each point being within approximately a day's car journey from the one selected. In this way it becomes possible to make one of these Key Points the headquarters for an exploratory tour of a day, a few days or a week. In Cornwall alone, for instance, there is material enough to occupy a whole holiday, and the same applies to Somerset, Wiltshire, South and North Wales, Dorset, Derbyshire, Cumbria, Lothian and the Roman Walls.

It is natural that the regions covered by the Key Points may overlap but with the map and a little judgement it should be possible to select convenient bases.

LONDON, KENT, SURREY, SUSSEX (Map 7)
Key points **London, Canterbury, Bognor Regis, Worthing**
Bignor Roman Villa, Sussex (p. 160); Caburn hill-fort, East Sussex (p. 84); Chanctonbury Ring hill-fort, West Sussex (p. 92); Cissbury hill-fort, West Sussex (p. 93); Coldrum chambered long barrow, Kent (p. 94); Dover Roman pharos, Kent (p. 143); Fishbourne Roman villa, Sussex (p. 162); Frensham Common bowl barrows, Surrey (p. 108); Kits Coty chambered long barrow, Kent (p. 120); London sites (pp. 122–3); Lullingstone Roman villa, Kent (p. 163); Oldbury hill-fort, Kent (p. 131); Pevensey Roman fort of the Saxon Shore, East Sussex (p. 144); Reculver Roman fort of the Saxon Shore, Kent (p. 143); Richborough Roman fort of the Saxon Shore, Kent (p. 143); West Sussex flint mines near Findon (p. 128).

BERKSHIRE, BUCKINGHAMSHIRE, OXFORDSHIRE (Map 6)

Key points **Aylesbury, Oxford, Reading**

Bulstrode Camp hill-fort, Buckinghamshire (p. 83); Cholesbury Camp hill-fort, Buckinghamshire (p. 93); Lambourn barrow cemetery, Berkshire (p. 121); North Leigh Roman villa, Oxfordshire (p. 164); The Rollright Stones, Oxfordshire (p. 135); Uffington Castle and White Horse, Berkshire (p. 175); Wayland's Smithy chambered long barrow, Berkshire (p. 175).

BEDFORDSHIRE, CAMBRIDGESHIRE, ESSEX, HERTFORDSHIRE, NORFOLK, SUFFOLK (Map 7)

Key points **St Albans, Cambridge, Colchester, Norwich**

Ambresbury Banks hill-fort, Essex (p. 62); The Bartlow Hills Roman barrows, Essex (p. 136); Bradwell Roman fort of the Saxon Shore, Essex (p. 142); Burgh Castle Roman fort of the Saxon Shore, Norfolk (p. 142); Caistor-by-Norwich Roman town, Norfolk (p. 154); Caister-by-Yarmouth Roman town, Norfolk (p. 154); Car Dyke Roman canal, Cambridgeshire (p. 86); Colchester Roman town, Essex (p. 156); Grimes Graves flint mines, Norfolk (p. 128); Holkham lowland fort, Norfolk (p. 118); Mersea Island Roman barrow, Essex (p. 136); St Albans Roman town, Hertfordshire (p. 158); Warham lowland fort, Norfolk (p. 175).

AVON, DORSET, SOMERSET (Map 3)

Key points **Bristol, Dorchester, Taunton, Weymouth**

Ackling Dyke Roman road, Dorset (p. 151); Aveline's Hole, Avon (p. 89); Badbury Rings hill-fort, Dorset (p. 75); Bath Roman town, Avon (p. 153); Bindon Hill promontory fort, Dorset (p. 77); Bristol hill-forts, Avon; Blaise Castle, Borough Walls, Clifton Down, Kings Weston, Stokeleigh (pp. 79–80); Buzbury Rings hill-fort, Dorset (p. 84); Cadbury Castle hill-fort, Somerset (p. 84); The Cerne Giant, Dorset (p. 92); Charterhouse-on-Mendip mining settlement, Avon (p. 127); The Cheddar Gorge (p. 89); Deverel barrow, Dorset (p. 103); Dorchester Roman town, Dorset (p. 156); The Dorset Cursus and neighbouring sites: Wor Barrow long barrow, Thickthorn long barrows, Knowlton Circles, Oakley Down barrow cemetery, Bokerley Dyke (pp. 103–5); Eggardon hill-fort, Dorset (p. 106); Ham Hill hill-fort, Somerset (p. 115);

10

Hambledon Hill causewayed camp and hill-fort, Dorset (p. 115); Hengistbury Head promontory fort, Dorset (p. 117); Hod Hill hill-fort and Roman fort, Dorset (p. 117); Keynsham Somerdale Roman villa, Avon (p. 163); Kings Weston Roman villa, Avon (p. 163); Maiden Castle causewayed camp and hill-fort, Dorset (p. 125); Nine Barrows, Dorset (p. 129); Nine Stones, Dorset (p. 129); Pimperne long barrow, Dorset (p. 134); Priddy Circles, Somerset (p. 134); Stanton Drew sacred sites, Avon (p. 167); Stoney Littleton chambered long barrow, Avon (p. 172); Wookey Hole, Somerset (p. 91); Worlebury hill-fort, Avon (p. 178).

HAMPSHIRE, ISLE OF WIGHT, WILTSHIRE (Map 5)
Key points **Andover, Basingstoke, Devizes, Salisbury, Winchester**
Avebury and neighbouring sites, Wiltshire: Avebury circles, Kennet Avenue, The Sanctuary, West Kennet Long Barrow, Silbury Hill, The Long Stones, Windmill Hill (pp. 71–5); Barbury Castle, Wiltshire (p. 76); Brading Roman villa, Isle of Wight (p. 161); Danebury hill-fort, Hampshire (p. 102); Fyfield and Overton Downs Celtic Fields, Wiltshire (p. 108); Knap Hill causewayed camp and enclosure, Wiltshire (p. 120); Portchester Roman fort of the Saxon Shore, Hampshire (p. 144); St Catherine's Hill hill-fort, Hampshire (p. 166); Silchester Roman town, Hampshire (p. 159); Snail Down barrow cemetery, Wiltshire (p. 166); Stonehenge and its neighbourhood: Stonehenge, Durrington Walls sacred site, Normanton Down barrow cemetery, Winterbourne Cross-roads barrow cemetery, Woodhenge (pp. 169–172); Yarnbury Castle hill-fort, Wiltshire (p. 178).

CORNWALL, DEVON (Maps 1 and 2)
Key points **Launceston, Penzance, Wadebridge**
Blackbury Castle hill-fort, Devon (p. 78); Broad Down barrow cemetery, Devon (p. 80); Carn Brea hill-fort and hut village, Cornwall (p. 87); Castle an Dinas hill-fort, Cornwall (p. 87); Cornwall West: Ballowal chambered round barrow, Boscawen-Un stone circle, Carn Euny village and fogou, Chapel Euny chambered long barrow, Chun Castle hill-fort, Chun Quoit chambered tomb, Chysauster village, Lanyon Quoit, Men an Tol, The Merry Maidens, Mulfra Quoit, Treryn (Treen) Dinas, Zennor Quoit (pp. 94–100); Halligye

11

fogou, Cornwall (p. 114); Harlyn Bay cemetery, Cornwall (p. 115); Hembury causewayed camp and hill-fort, Devon (p. 115); The Hurlers stone circles, Cornwall (p. 118); Kent's Cavern, Devon (p. 90); Kestor village settlement, Devon (p. 119); Martinhoe Roman fort and signal station, Devon (p. 141); Merrivale stone rows, Devon (p. 126); Old Burrow Roman fort and signal station, Devon (p. 141); Rillaton round barrow, Cornwall (p. 134); Scorhill stone circle, Devon (p. 166); Trethevy Quoit, Cornwall (p. 174).

GLOUCESTERSHIRE, GWENT, HEREFORD AND WORCESTER (Map 5)
Key points **Cheltenham, Caerleon, Hereford, Worcester**
Aconbury hill-fort, Hereford and Worcester (p. 62); Arthur's Stone chambered long barrow, Hereford and Worcester (p. 71); Bagendon earthworks, Gloucestershire (p. 75); Belas Knap chambered long barrow, Gloucestershire (p. 77); Blackpool Bridge Roman road, Gloucestershire (p. 151); Bredon Hill promontory fort, Hereford and Worcester (p. 78); The Bulwarks earthworks, Gloucestershire (p. 83); Caerleon Roman legionary fort, Gwent (p. 148); Caerwent Roman town, Gwent (p. 154); Chedworth Roman villa, Gloucestershire (p. 161); Cirencester Roman town, Gloucestershire (p. 155); Conderton Camp, Hereford and Worcester (p. 94); Croft Ambry hill-fort, Hereford and Worcester (p. 100); Gatcombe Lodge chambered long barrow, Gloucestershire (p. 108); Great Witcombe Roman villa, Gloucestershire (p. 163); Hetty Pegler's Tump chambered long barrow, Gloucestershire (p. 117); Leckhampton Hill promontory fort, Gloucestershire (p. 122); Lydney hill-fort, mines and Roman temple, Gloucestershire (p. 124); Midsummer and Hollybush Hills hill-fort, Hereford and Worcester (p. 127); Notgrove long barrow, Gloucestershire (p. 130); Nympsfield chambered long barrow, Gloucestershire (p. 130); Sutton Walls hill-fort, Hereford and Worcester (p. 172); Woodchester Roman villa, Gloucestershire (p. 165).

LEICESTERSHIRE, NORTHAMPTONSHIRE, STAFFORDSHIRE, WARWICKSHIRE, WEST MIDLANDS (Map 6)
Key points **Leamington Spa, Leicester, Lichfield**
Leicester Roman town (p. 158); Oldbury Camp hill-fort,

Arthur's Stone, Dorstone, Hereford and Worcester

Silchester from the air (central rectangular area)

Warwickshire (p. 131); Rainsborough Camp, Northamptonshire (p. 134); Thor's Cave rock shelter, Staffordshire (p. 90);
Wall Roman town, Staffordshire (p. 160).

DERBYSHIRE, LINCOLNSHIRE, NOTTINGHAMSHIRE (Map 8)

Key points **Matlock, Newark, Lincoln**

Arbor Low sacred site, Derbyshire (p. 70); Creswell Crags
rock shelters, Derbyshire (p. 90); Five Wells chambered
tomb, Derbyshire (p. 107); Green Low chambered tomb,
Derbyshire (p. 108); Hob Hurst's House, Derbyshire (p. 117);
Horncastle Roman town, Lincolnshire (p. 157); Lincoln
Roman town (p. 158); Oxton Camp hill-fort, Nottinghamshire (p. 132); Stanton Moor cairn cemetery, Derbyshire
(p. 168).

DYFED, GLAMORGAN (WEST, MID AND SOUTH), POWYS (Map 4)

Key points **Llandovery, Lampeter** (for Dolaucothi); **Newport** (Dyfed, for Pentre Ifan); **Brecon, Cardiff, Porthcawl,
Llanelly**

Brecon Gaer Roman fort, Powys (p. 137); Cardiff Castle
Roman fort, South Glamorgan (p. 138); Coelbren Roman fort,
West Glamorgan (p. 138); Dolaucothi gold mines, Dyfed (p.
127); Gelligaer Roman fort, Mid-Glamorgan (p. 139); Parc-le-
Breos chambered long barrow, West Glamorgan (p. 132);
Pentre Ifan chambered long barrow, Dyfed (p. 132); St
Lythan's chambered long barrow, South Glamorgan (p. 166);
Tinkinswood chambered long barrow, South Glamorgan
(p. 173).

CHESHIRE, CLWYD, GWYNEDD, SALOP (Maps 1 and 4)

Key points **Chester, Holyhead, Caernarvon**

The Anglesey sites, Gwynedd: Barclodiad y gawres passage
grave (p. 64), Bodowyr burial chamber (p. 64), Bryn celli ddu
passage grave (p. 65), Caer Gybi Roman fort (p. 137), Caer
Leb earthwork (p. 66), Caer y twyr hill-fort (p. 66), Castell
Bryn Gwyn defensive site (p. 66), Din Lligwy walled homestead (p. 66), Holyhead Mountain hut circles (p. 67), Lligwy
burial chamber (p. 67), Penrhos Feilw standing stones (p. 67),
Trefignath burial chamber (p. 67); Bridestones chambered

long barrow, Cheshire (p. 79); Burrow Camp and Bury Ditches hill-forts, Salop (p. 83); Caer Caradoc hill-fort, Salop (p. 85); Caernarvon Roman fort, Gwynedd (p. 138); Capel Garmon chambered long barrow, Gwynedd (p. 86); Caynham hill-fort, Salop (p. 91); Chester legionary fort (p. 149); Mitchell's Fold stone circle, Salop (p. 129); Old Oswestry hill-fort, Salop (p. 131); The Wrekin hill-fort, Salop (p. 178); Wroxeter Roman town, Salop (p. 160).

HUMBERSIDE, YORKSHIRE (WEST, NORTH AND SOUTH) (Map 8)
Key points **York, Malton, Scarborough, Harrogate, Grassington**

Aldborough Roman town, North Yorkshire (p. 153); Almondbury hill-fort, West Yorkshire (p. 62); Blackstone Edge Roman road, West Yorkshire (p. 152); Cawthorn Roman practice camps, North Yorkshire (p. 91); Danby Rigg monuments, North Yorkshire (p. 101); Danes' Graves barrow cemetery, Humberside (p. 102); Devil's Arrows standing stones, North Yorkshire (p. 103); Duggleby Howe round barrow, North Yorkshire (p. 106); Goldsborough Roman fort and signal station, North Yorkshire (p. 139); Ilkley Moor and Baildon Hill stone circles, cairns and carvings, West Yorkshire (p. 118); Ingleborough hill-fort, North Yorkshire (p. 118); Scarborough Roman fort and signal station, North Yorkshire (p. 142); Stanwick fortified site, North Yorkshire (p. 168); Thornborough, Hutton Moor and Cana sacred sites, North Yorkshire (p. 173); Victoria Cave, North Yorkshire (p. 91); Wade's Causeway Roman road, North Yorkshire (p. 152); York legionary fort (p. 150).

CUMBRIA, DUMFRIES AND GALLOWAY, LANCASHIRE (Map 9)
Key points **Lancaster, Morecambe, Penrith, Carlisle**

Bewcastle Roman frontier fort, Cumbria (p. 145); Birrens Roman frontier fort, Dumfries and Galloway (p. 145); Burnswark Roman frontier fort, Dumfries and Galloway (p. 145); Castle How hill-fort, Cumbria (p. 87); Castlerigg stone circle, Cumbria (p. 88); Crosby village settlements, Cumbria (p. 101); Eskdale Moor stone circles, Cumbria (p. 107);

Hadrian's Wall (west end) and forts, Cumbria (pp. 109–114); Hardknott Roman fort, Cumbria (p. 139); King Arthur's Round Table and Mayborough sacred sites, Cumbria (p. 119); Lacra stone circles, Cumbria (p. 121); Long Meg and her Daughters stone circle, Cumbria (p. 124); Maiden Castle Roman fort, Cumbria (p. 140); Pike of Stickle axe factory, Cumbria (p. 128); Ribchester Roman fort, Lancashire (p. 141); Walls Castle Roman bath-house, Cumbria (p. 142).

CLEVELAND, DURHAM, NORTHUMBERLAND TYNE AND WEAR (Map 9)
Key points **Morpeth, Alnwick**

Duddo Stone Circle, Northumberland (p. 105); Hadrian's Wall and forts (centre and east) Northumberland (pp. 109–114); High Rochester Roman frontier fort, Northumberland (p. 146); Piercebridge Roman fort, Durham (p. 141); Risingham Roman frontier fort, Northumberland (p. 146); Rothbury cairns and hill-forts, Northumberland (p. 165); South Shields Roman frontier fort, Tyne and Wear (p. 147); Wooler cairns, settlements and hill-forts, Northumberland (p. 177).

BORDERS, LOTHIAN (Map 10)
Key points **Edinburgh, Galashiels, Dunbar**

The Antonine Wall (pp. 68–9); Cairnpapple henge and cairn, Lothian (p. 86); Castle Law hill-fort, Lothian (p. 88); Chesters hill-fort, Lothian (p. 92); Crichton souterrain, Lothian (p. 100); Dreva hill-fort, Borders (p. 105); Edinburgh sites, Lothian (p. 106); Edinshall broch, Borders (p. 81); Eildon Hill hill-fort and Roman signal station, Borders (p. 107); Lyne Roman frontier fort, Borders (p. 146); Mutiny stones, Borders (p. 129); Torwoodlee fort and broch, Borders (p. 82); Traprain Law hill-fort, Lothian (p. 174); Woden Law hill-fort and Roman siege works, Borders (p. 176).

CENTRAL, FIFE, TAYSIDE (Map 10)
Key points **Stirling, Perth, Montrose**

The Antonine Wall (pp. 68–9); Ardestie souterrain, Tayside (p. 70); Ardoch Roman frontier fort, Tayside (p. 144); The Caterthuns forts, Tayside (p. 89); Fendoch Roman frontier fort, Tayside (p. 145); Finavon vitrified fort, Tayside (p. 107); Inchtuthil legionary fort, Tayside (p. 149); Normans Law hill-fort, Fife (p. 130); Tappoch broch, Central (p. 82).

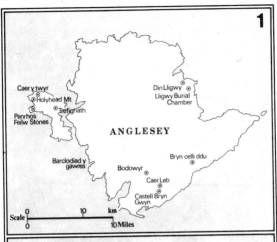

1

Caer y twyr
Holyhead Mt
Penrhos
Feilw Stones
Trefignath

Din Lligwy
Lligwy Burial
Chamber

ANGLESEY

Bryn celli ddu

Barclodiad y
gawres

Bodowyr

Caer Leb

Castell Bryn
Gwyn

Scale
0 — 10 — km
0 — 10 Miles

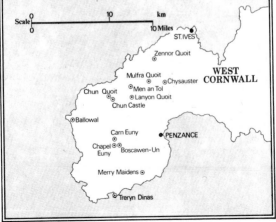

Scale
0 — 10 — km
0 — 10 Miles

ST. IVES

Zennor Quoit

**WEST
CORNWALL**

Mulfra Quoit
Chysauster
Chun Quoit
Men an Tol
Lanyon Quoit
Chun Castle

Ballowal

Carn Euny
PENZANCE
Chapel
Euny
Boscawen-Un

Merry Maidens

Treryn Dinas

17

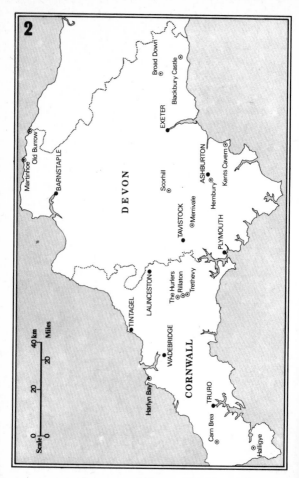

18

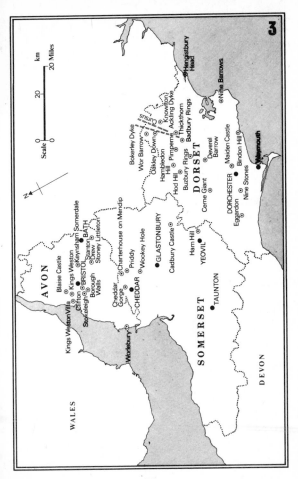

19

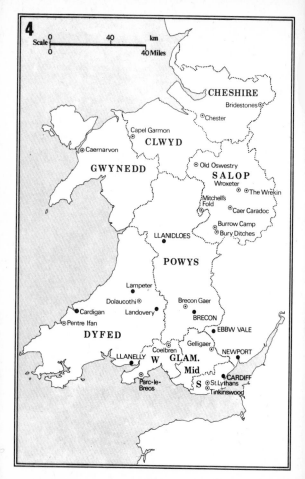

4

Scale

0   40   km

0   40 Miles

CHESHIRE

Bridestones⊙

⊙ Chester

Capel Garmon ⊙

CLWYD

⊙ Caernarvon

GWYNEDD

⊙ Old Oswestry

SALOP

Wroxeter
⊙   ⊙ The Wrekin

Mitchell's
Fold ⊙
    ⊙ Caer Caradoc

⊙ Burrow Camp
⊙ Bury Ditches

LLANIDLOES ●

POWYS

Lampeter ⊙

Dolaucothi ⊙   Brecon Gaer ⊙
   Landovery

● Cardigan

⊙ Pentre Ifan

DYFED

BRECON

⊙ EBBW VALE

Coelbren   Gelligaer ⊙   NEWPORT

LLANELLY   **W**   **GLAM.**

Mid

⊙ CARDIFF

⊙ Parc-le-
Breos

S   ⊙ St.Lythans
     ⊙ Tinkinswood

20

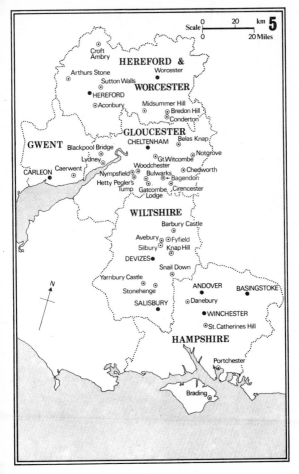

Scale 0 — 20 km
0 — 20 Miles

5

Croft
Ambry ⊙

HEREFORD &
⊙ Arthurs Stone ● Worcester
⊙ Sutton Walls **WORCESTER**
● HEREFORD
⊙ Aconbury ⊙ Midsummer Hill
⊙ Bredon Hill
⊙ Conderton

GLOUCESTER
GWENT Blackpool Bridge ● CHELTENHAM ⊙ Belas Knap
⊙ Lydney ⊙ Gt.Witcombe ⊙ Notgrove
CARLEON ● Caerwent ● Woodchester ⊙ Chedworth
Nympsfield ⊙ Bulwarks
Hetty Pegler's ⊙ Bagendon
Tump Gatcombe ⊙ Cirencester
Lodge

WILTSHIRE
Barbury Castle ⊙
Avebury ⊙ ⊙ Fyfield
Silbury ⊙ Knap Hill ⊙
DEVIZES ●
Snail Down ⊙
Yarnbury Castle ⊙
⊙ ● ANDOVER ● BASINGSTOKE
Stonehenge ⊙ Danebury
SALISBURY ● ● WINCHESTER
⊙ St.Catherines Hill

HAMPSHIRE

Portchester

Brading ⊙

N

21

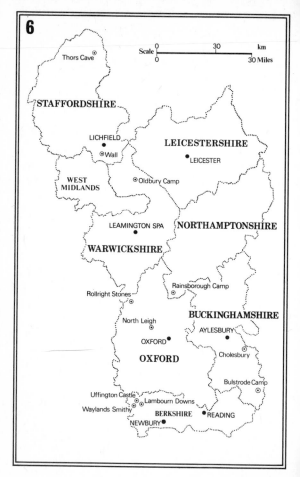

6

Scale
0 — 30 km
0 — 30 Miles

Thors Cave ⊙

STAFFORDSHIRE

LICHFIELD
●
⊙ Wall

LEICESTERSHIRE

LEICESTER ●

**WEST
MIDLANDS**

⊙ Oldbury Camp

NORTHAMPTONSHIRE

LEAMINGTON SPA ●

WARWICKSHIRE

Rainsborough Camp ⊙

Rollright Stones ⊙

BUCKINGHAMSHIRE

North Leigh ⊙

AYLESBURY ●

OXFORD ●

⊙ Cholesbury

OXFORD

Bulstrode Camp ⊙

Uffington Castle ⊙
⊙ Lambourn Downs
Waylands Smithy ⊙
BERKSHIRE ● READING
NEWBURY ●

22

8

Stanwick

NORTH YORKSHIRE

⊙ Goldsborough

Danby Rigg ⊙

⊙ Ingleborough

Wade's Causeway

⊙ Thornborough

Victoria Cave ⊙

Hutton Moor & Cana

Cawthorn Camps

SCARBOROUGH

GRASSINGTON ●

Aldborough

⊙ Devils Arrows

● **MALTON**

Ilkley Moor

HARROGATE ●

⊙ Duggleby Howe

YORK ●

⊙ Danes Graves

WEST YORKSHIRE Baildon Moor

HUMBERSIDE

⊙ Blackstone Edge

⊙ Almondbury

SOUTH YORKSHIRE

Five Wells ⊙

⊙ Creswell Crags

Arbor Low ⊙

LINCOLN ●

⊙ Stanton Moor

Green Low ⊙

NOTTINGHAMSHIRE

⊙ Horncastle

Oxton Camp ⊙

DERBYSHIRE

● **NEWARK**

LINCOLNSHIRE

Scale 0 — 40 — km
0 — 20 — 40 Miles

N

24

25

PRINCIPAL SITES OUTSIDE THE AREA OF ROMAN PENETRATION

Some of the following may be long distances from large centres of population but, for those holidaying in their neighbourhood, may be worth a visit. They are given here in their counties in alphabetical order. For convenience their former county is entered in brackets where necessary.

DUMFRIES AND GALLOWAY
Barsalloch Point Iron Age hill-fort, 1 mile (1.6 km) NE of Monreith (Wigtownshire).

Boreland neolithic chambered cairn, 2 miles (3.2 km) N of Newton Stewart (Kircudbright).

Burrow Head Iron Age promontory fort, 5 miles (8 km) SW of Isle of Whithorn (Wigtownshire).

Cairnholy neolithic horned chambered cairn (DE), 6½ miles (10.5 km) SE of Creetown (Kirkcudbright).

Cauldside Bronze Age cairns and stone circle, 5 miles (8 km) ESE of Creetown (Kircudbright).

Doon of May Iron Age vitrified fort, 10 miles (16 km) SE of Glenluce, S of Loch Mochrum (Wigtownshire).

Glenquicken Bronze Age stone circle, 3 miles (4.8 km) E of Creetown (Kircudbright).

GRAMPIAN
Barmekin of Echt Iron Age hill-fort, 1 mile (1.6 km) NW of Echt (Aberdeen).

Cullerlie Stone (DE), Bronze Age stone circle, 10 miles (16 km) W of Aberdeen.

27

Jarlshof, Shetland

Dunnideer Iron Age vitrified fort, 2 miles (3.2 km) W of Insch (Aberdeen).

Easter Aquorthies (DE), Bronze Age stone circle, 4 miles (6.4 km) W of Inverurie (Aberdeen).

Loanhead of Daviot (DE), Bronze Age recumbent stone circle and ring cairn, 2 miles (3.2 km) NW of Daviot (Aberdeen).

Longman Cairn, neolithic long cairn, at Longmanhill, 5 miles (8 km) SE of Banff.

Memsie Bronze Age stone circle (DE), 1 mile (1.6 km) S of Memsie (Aberdeen).

Tomnaverie Bronze Age stone circle (DE), 5 miles (8 km) NE of Dinnet (Aberdeen).

HIGHLANDS

An Sgurr Iron Age hill-fort on the island of Eigg.

Clava Cairns (DE), neolithic chambered cairns and ring cairn, 6 miles (9.6 km) E of Inverness.

Cnoc Freidacain neolithic chambered cairns (DE), Dorrery (Caithness).

Coille na Borgie neolithic long-horned chambered cairns, 3 miles (4.8 km) S of Bettyhill (Sutherland).

Corriemony neolithic chambered cairn (DE) in Glen Urquhart (Inverness).

Dun Lagaidh Iron Age vitrified fort and Dun an Ruigh Ruadh Iron Age broch on S side of Loch Broom SSE of Ullapool.

The Glenelg Iron Age brochs (DE): Dun Troddan, 3 miles (4.8 km) SE of Glenelg, and Dun Telve (DE), 2 miles (3.2 km) S of Glenelg.

Grey Cairns of Camster (DE), neolithic round horned cairn, 9 miles N of Lybster (Caithness).

Kinrive neolithic chambered cairn, 7 miles (11.3 km) N of Invergordon (Ross and Cromarty).

Knockfarell Iron Age vitrified fort, 3 miles (4.8 km) W of Dingwall (Ross and Cromarty).

Millcraig neolithic chambered cairn, 5 miles (8 km) NW of Invergordon (Ross and Cromarty).

ISLE OF LEWIS
Callanish Bronze Age Stone circles, cairns, stone avenue (DE).

Dun Carloway Iron Age broch (DE).

Steinacleit neolithic chambered cairn (DE).

ORKNEY ISLANDS
Dwarfie Stone (DE) on Hoy, immediately S of Ward Hill, 2 miles (3.2 km) from coast; an enormous boulder with a tunnel cut into its side and made into a neolithic rock-cut tomb.

Kirkwall group of monuments: Cuween Hill neolithic chambered tomb (DE), 6 miles (9.7 km) W of Kirkwall. Grain souterrain (DE) just NW of Kirkwall. Maes Howe neolithic chambered cairn (DE) in Stenness parish a few yards from Kirkwall-Stromness Road. Onston (or Unstan) chambered cairn (DE) on a spit of land projecting into Loch of Stenness. Rennibister souterrain (DE) at Rennibister Farm, 4 miles (6.4 km) W of Kirkwall. Ring of Brogar Bronze Age stone circle (DE) between lochs of Harray and Stenness. Stones of Stenness (DE), near Bridge of Brogar, part of a stone circle with a standing stone. Wideford Hill Cairns (DE), just W of Kirkwall.

Mid Howe broch and chambered cairn (DE) on W coast of Isle of Rousay.

Skara Brae hut village (DE) on W coast of mainland in Bay of Skaill. One of the most important prehistoric sites in Britain.

(Visitors are recommended to obtain the HMSO booklets on Orkney, Skara Brae, Maes Howe etc.)

SHETLAND ISLES
Clickhimin broch (DE) on south shore of Clickhimin Loch $\frac{1}{4}$ mile (1.2 km) S of Lerwick; a fine example of

Two views of Skara Brae, Orkney

a broch which developed from a farmstead and later became a wheelhouse with partition walls arranged like the spokes of a wheel.

Jarlshof Bronze and Iron Age settlements (DE) on extreme southern point of mainland; a complicated series of habitations with huts, souterrains and a broch. A very important site.

Mousa broch (DE) on Isle of Mousa, 15 miles (24.1 km) S of Lerwick opposite Sandwick; one of the best preserved of all brochs.

(Visitors are advised to obtain HMSO handbooks.)

STRATHCLYDE

Auchgallon Bronze Age stone circle (DE), Isle of Arran.

Cairnbaan Bronze Age cup and ring marked stones (DE) (Argyll).

Dunagoil vitrified fort (DE) (Bute).

Kilmichael Glassary Bronze Age cup and ring marked stones (DE) (Argyll).

Poltalloch Monuments (DE): cairns, standing stones, cup and ring marked rocks etc. (Argyll).

Tormore neolithic burial chamber, Isle of Arran.

Stonehenge, Wiltshire

ANCIENT BRITAIN,
A BRIEF HISTORICAL OUTLINE

In Great Britain there are thousands of sites, some isolated on mountains and moorland, others in city streets or hidden in the basements of more modern buildings, which reveal how our forbears lived, worked, fought, died and were buried. Some, like Stonehenge, stand out as landmarks; others may be walked over or passed by without notice. Many are invisible on the ground and have only been discovered from the air during the last 50 years as lines, rectangles and circles of a lighter colour among growing crops or grass or corn. This book deals with some of the most important of these sites, their place in history and what they can show to the visitor.

From the earliest days man has been dependent on what resources the earth could offer him, and this is no less true today than it was when men of the Old Stone Age sought warmth and comfort in caves, chipped flints for weapons and when their women gathered nuts, roots and berries for food. The great difference between them and us is that today the land itself is being reshaped to serve mankind.

We are no longer, as they were making use of what is there on the spot. With our huge machines we are taking and transporting it, changing its form, making artificial hills and tracks, drowning valleys, reclaiming land from the sea, altering the courses of rivers to an extent never dreamed of even half a century ago. In the process of roadmaking, foundation-digging and the like, evidences of the past are being obliterated at an ever-increasing rate, and archaeologists are hard pressed to get leave even for a few days' exploration before the mechanical diggers and bulldozers are brought in and tons of earth with whatever relics they contain, are shifted. Nobody travelling in Europe or, for that matter, in many other parts of the world can fail to notice how cement and steel are changing its aspect. Local differences in materials, methods and ways of life are disappearing, and one centre of population is becoming at first glance, very much like another.

To all this there has been a reaction. The speed of destruction and reconstruction has made us more conscious of what visible remains there are of man's past on these islands. Through the press, the radio and television, archaeology, once the province of the few, has captured the imagination of the general public. More and more people are ready to spend weekends and holidays on 'digs' and to undertake expeditions to find evidence of man's origin and unwritten history. Museums are attracting visitors bent not only on seeing, but also on knowing. Popular books and guides are appearing in increasing numbers. One sinister aspect of all this is the rising cash value of ancient pieces of pottery, metalwork and sculpture, which has encouraged the robbing of sites and the consequent destruction of valuable evidence.

THE PALAEOLITHIC OR OLD STONE AGE

Between 500,000 and 200,000 years ago Great Britain was given something like its present configuration by the great ice sheets which formed over its northern and western parts during four successive cold periods, collectively known as the Ice Age. During that time the ice gave form to the mountain groups and ranges, and in the warm intervals between the glaciations or great frosts, the volume of water caused by melting ice brought about flooding and the consequent rise in the sea level. These processes carved out the valleys, spreading soil and debris over the lowlands.

Creatures bearing some resemblance to man were living in East Anglia in the warm interval after the second of these glaciations round about 400,000 years BC. Their weapons and implements of flaked flint have been found at Clacton and other places, and they were the first of a series of cultures which produced more of such weapons and tools, found in caves and rock shelters in various parts of the country. The age in which they lived, lasting until about 10,000 BC—a vast length of time, is called the Old Stone (or Palaeolithic) Age. It is represented in England by Creswell Crags (Derbyshire), Kents Cavern (Devon), King Arthur's Cave (Hereford and Worcester), Cheddar and Wookey (Somerset), among others. During the later (or Upper) Palaeolithic Age these people had learnt to make fire, to adapt the skins of animals for clothing, to tame the dog and probably to put up temporary shelters made from the boughs of trees. These arts and the making of tools from flint and bone represented the first steps towards man's control of his environment.

Some 15,000 years before the birth of Christ the last ice sheets gradually retreated and the landscape of Britain underwent another fundamental change. The sub-arctic vegetation retreated with the ice and was replaced by dense growths of forests with birch, pine, hazel, elms and oaks. Man emerged from the Ice Age with increased possibilities. His mastery of flint-chipping techniques had produced fine small heads for arrows and spears; his sharper axe and adze, set in their wooden hafts made possible the building of better huts, of boats, paddles and other useful articles. He was able to leave the caves for prolonged periods and to venture into more open sites, living as a hunter and fisher. As a result the population increased greatly. Thus passed the comparatively short Middle Stone (or Mesolithic) Age. At some time during this period, probably between 6000 and 5000 BC, the sea flowed into the marshland which lay between this country and what is now France, the Netherlands and Germany. Land which had for ages been passable marsh, studded with lagoons, over which incomers had been able to come on foot, was turned into two stretches of water—the North Sea and the English Channel—giving England its east and south coasts.

Apart from his fine implements of flint and bone, Mesolithic man has left few remains. One of the places where they have been found above the bones of elephant, hippopotamus, woolly rhinoceros, deer, bear and fox, is Victoria Cave near Settle in North Yorkshire. In other parts of England their presence has been revealed by the odd discovery of a few small flints or bone implements in inhabited caves and pit shelters. These places were apparently used for short periods as, in pursuit of a means of livelihood, men moved with the changing seasons to more convenient homes.

THE NEOLITHIC OR NEW STONE AGE

The separation of Britain from the Continent did not stop the migration of peoples. Some time after about 3500 BC there were new arrivals, probably of people in small groups and taking place over a long period. These, coming mainly from what are now France and the Netherlands, spread over the lowland areas of Britain from Cornwall to East Yorkshire, overcoming and eventually mingling with the native peoples. With them they brought new weapons and tools—stone axes, symmetrically shaped by grinding, an entirely new process. Their flint knives, scrapers, spear- and arrow-heads were also finely finished. For this reason the age in which they lived in England, roughly up to the date 2000 BC, has been called the Neolithic or New Stone Age.

The neolithic people, however, brought far more than the polished stone tool. In the Near and Middle East mankind had already learnt the rudiments of farming and had taken to sowing and cultivating a primitive form of wheat known as *emmer*. The domestication of animals, cattle in particular, increased man's power to till the soil as well as freeing him from the necessity of food-gathering and hunting as his main means of livelihood. Thus, on the well-drained soils of Britain, especially on the chalk downlands of Wessex and on some of the river gravels, these people set up their first mixed farms. With their improved tools they were better able to hew down trees and make clearings on the edge of woodland and forest. In these clearings they would, for a few seasons, sow seeds and gather in their harvests, moving on to fresh sites when the productivity of the land at last gave out.

Through these discoveries alone, neolithic man became able to live a far more settled and secure life. The increased control of the food supply made it possible for both men and women to carry on domestic crafts such as pottery, basket-making, leatherwork, carpentry, the making of boats, the weaving of simple fabrics and the plaiting of ropes. To a certain extent some specialization must have taken place involving

37

Axe-head and flint weapons

the exchange of skills for food, and we know that over the whole country, trade in flints and flint weapons and tools was carried on. Axes made from stone and mined in the Lake District have been found in East Anglia, and implements from the Prescelly Mountains in Wales or fashioned from *whin sill*, a hard rock found only in northern England, have appeared in the south-west.

In the early neolithic period all the flint for tools and weapons was found on or near the surface. At Pike of Stickle in Cumbria and at Craig Lwyd, Penmaenmawr in Wales, waste flakes, roughed-out axe-heads and hammer-stones can still be picked up as they lie on the slopes, for there was always considerable waste in the making of good flint tools. Later, flint-mining became a major industry. At Grimes Graves in Norfolk 34 acres (13.7 ha) of mine workings are still to be seen, with shafts driven deep underground and galleries radiating from them. Flints from this area were exported all over the country. Some people have alluded to this remarkable advance from a hunting and food-gathering population to one of farmers and stock-rearers as the Neolithic Revolution.

We know little of the kind of settlement or dwelling in which these people lived. The site of an open village since deserted must have been overgrown by heath and scrub, leaving only lost or castaway stone tools, fragments of pottery and domestic rubbish as evidence. They did, however, throw up the earliest earthworks to have survived—the so-called *causewayed camps*, which they probably used for the herding of cattle and as protection from wild animals. These enclosures were roughly circular in shape, and were surrounded by one or more ditches and banks. Their name comes from the gaps in the ditches over which level paths or causeways led to the entrances. Nearly a dozen of these have been traced in southern England, by far the largest being Windmill Hill near Avebury in Wiltshire. The wealth of objects recovered from this site has given a name to the type of culture in which farming played so large a part.

An increase in production must have brought about many changes, among them an increase in population. It has been suggested on a calculation based on the number of probable settlements that the population of the Wessex chalkland alone in the early neolithic period was at least 4000, more than one per square kilometre. This alone would mean that prehistoric man had gone far towards the creation of social units and probably towards the evolution of a ruling class or aristocracy. What is left of the enormous stone monuments of the period goes to bear this out.

There were, first of all, the long barrows. Southwest England has the largest number, but there are others in Sussex, Wales, Lincolnshire, East Yorkshire and even as far north as the Lake District and southern Scotland. They were long mounds of earth or stone piled up in the same way as the ramparts of the causewayed camps. The simplest barrows covered small wooden constructions in each of which large numbers of bones had been placed, sometimes those of as many as fifty persons. It appears that the neolithic people were accustomed to keep the remains of their most important persons for months or even years in special huts or enclosures until enough had been accumulated to bury them *en masse*. They probably did not have the same qualms about keeping decaying corpses above ground as we do. Once the interment had been concluded, with what ceremonies we do not know, and the great mound of earth had been piled on top of it, the tomb or barrow was closed and remained as a monument. Ditches were dug along both sides of the long mound of earth and these were sometimes brought together at one end to join in a semicircle. This kind of earthen long barrow is found on the downland from Dorset to Sussex, in Lincolnshire and East Yorkshire, and may be anything from 90 to 150 ft (27.4 to 45.7 m) long and up to 12 ft (3.7 m) high.

Other and more elaborate burial-places were the long or sometimes circular barrows which had been piled up over burial chambers built out of large blocks of stone. In some, called passage graves, the circular

Typical round barrow near Winterbourne, Dorset

Chambered barrow, Sancreed, Cornwall

tomb was approached by way of a long passage and may have had smaller chambers opening out of it. In others, called gallery graves, the long chamber or gallery was itself divided or opened out on to smaller chambers on each side, in which separate inter-ments were made. In the case of these 'chambered' barrows, there was no need to keep corpses for long periods, for the barrow could be opened and closed again when needed. Large numbers are to be found in Gloucestershire, north Wiltshire and Wales. In some cases the covering mounds have disappeared, leaving the large stones which enclosed the burial-chamber still standing, sometimes with the covering-stone or capstone still in position. Of these there are examples called *quoits* in Cornwall and others in Wales.

Burial in this kind of tomb points not only to the existence of an aristocracy among neolithic peoples, but also to the certainty that elaborate ritual practices existed among them, connected not only with death but also probably with other major events in life. Their religious beliefs must have had to do with the construction of what we call *secondary earthworks*, the cursus and the henge. Of these the former is an avenue varying in length from a few hundred yards to 6 miles (9.7 km), lying between two parallel banks with external ditches. Some of these cursuses are no longer visible on the ground and, like Thornborough Cursus in North Yorkshire, can only be seen from the air. The Dorset Cursus, 6 miles (9.7 km) long, is visible on the ground throughout the greater part of its length, and at one point near its southern end a long barrow stands across its path. It is the longest ceremonial earthwork in Britain, enclosing 220 acres (89 ha) and it has been estimated that with the tools then used, the task of completing it could have taken 100 men 2 years, assuming that they worked 10 hours a day and 7 days a week.

The second type of ceremonial earthwork is the henge. This consists of an area, roughly oval or circular, enclosed by one or more banks and ditches, with entrance gaps between them like those of the causewayed camp. Within the area enclosed there may be stone circles. Most henges have one, but Avebury has two large ones besides several smaller settings of stones. These henges vary greatly in size. One at Arminghall in Norfolk was only 90 ft (27.4 m) in diameter. Stonehenge is 380 ft (116 m), Avebury 1400 ft (426 m) and the lesser-known Durrington Walls, now almost invisible because of over-ploughing, 1600 ft (487 m).

What we see today are a few fragmentary remains of these stupendous structures. From reconstructions printed in guide-books it is possible for us to imagine what one of them must have been like with its circles of huge standing-stones and its regular well-kept ditch and bank, but to picture the aspect of the whole countryside dotted with long barrows, ceremonial henges and stone circles is almost beyond us. It is clear from descriptions that, in spite of the simplicity of their lives and the lack of what we would call modern amenities, these people were living well above subsistence level and were free to devote much of their energies to matters other than the mere provision of food, clothing and shelter. Though we know nothing about the nature of their ceremonies, the gods they worshipped or their religious lore, the size and character of their monuments, the pottery, weapons and tools found with their burials indicate that they were intensely preoccupied with the needs of man in the after-life. It surprises us more to know that, according to the most modern dating methods, Stonehenge and many other monuments of this age were constructed at and previous to 2000 BC, many centuries before the Israelites settled in the Holy Land and before the first glimmerings of western civilization appeared in ancient Greece.

Avebury from the air, showing henge

THE BRONZE AGE

One thing that should be understood about these remote days is that there were no such events as invasions in the sense that large numbers of people, organized and armed, descended on a country and took possession of it. What changes occurred were the results of the migration of small bands, families or clans, moving from one place to another and establishing themselves either by right of occupation or by force—a process of change in population and culture which could and often did take hundreds of years.

Such was the arrival in Britain of the 'Beaker People', whose migration is notable for the fact that they brought with them a type of pottery not seen before—the drinking cup or beaker. They appear to have been taller, stronger physically and more war-like than the native population, and their small bands were probably ruled by chieftains. Their weapons were still mainly of stone, though more advanced, the battle-axes of their chiefs being holed for attachment to the handles. They were also the first people on this island to use metal in the form of gold ornaments and copper knives, though there is no evidence that they smelted the copper they used. The first of these newcomers arrived from France and the Low Countries, settling in the eastern part of the island; later arrivals migrated into southern and western England, conquering and mingling with the native population.

After the coming of the Beaker people, burial customs gradually changed, communal interment in long barrows giving way to the burial of corpses singly in a crouching position under much smaller circular mounds called round barrows. Evidence of the transition from one type of burial to the other is to be found in odd places where two or more skeletons have been discovered with or without grave goods under a single circular mound.

The Beaker people had no inclination to build huge

monuments nor did they appear to pay much respect to those which already existed. Today we find neolithic henges and avenues with round burial mounds within the space between their ditches and dotted about the land around; we find Beaker-type burials in the sides of long barrows and in one place (Gorsey Bigbury, Somerset) a group of Beaker people had squatted in the ditch of a henge monument, lit fires, cooked their food and left behind fragments of nearly a hundred beakers.

Though these people used metal they can hardly be said to belong to the Bronze Age since they did not themselves smelt it. In Europe, however, the

Beakers

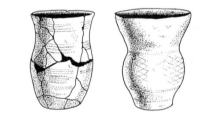

forging of tools and weapons of metal was taking place, while in south-western England and in Ireland rich sources of ore were being discovered. Again, the transition to the Bronze Age was not due to the large-scale migration of people, but rather to the spread of technical knowledge, possibly brought by itinerant smiths who travelled from one place to another, manufacturing their products on the spot. Thus in time the native populations, while they did not entirely give up the use of stone, became more and more dependent on metal.

The discovery of its extraction and use brought into being a change almost as fundamental in the structure of society as had been the neolithic revolution. It depended in the first place on the smith, the only man who knew how to extract the metal from the ore, and who had mastered the complicated process of fashioning it into tools and weapons. He was probably a member of a highly privileged society which included prospectors and workers. His secrets were jealously guarded and probably were also passed down from father to son. Secondly, it depended on the customer, the chieftain who relied on military power either to secure and retain his own position or to extend his dominions by war. Thirdly it depended on trade, the scope of which spread far and wide beyond the narrow confines of Britain. The search for, manufacture and use of bronze opened up the world from Scotland and Ireland to the continental coasts, concentrating economic and military power in the hands of the few much more than had been the case among the earlier neolithic communities.

The burial mounds and sacred monuments of the Bronze Age peoples are almost the only sources of information we have about them. These mounds, or round barrows, were of many kinds, and more than one kind may appear on the same site, as in the greater barrow cemeteries such as Snail Down (Wiltshire) and Oakley Down (Dorset). Great care was obviously taken in the siting of these monuments. Sometimes they are found in groups, sometimes in lines or crescents, and in hilly country they may be seen strung out along a prominent skyline as landmarks. In many cases they cluster round a larger long barrow or are in the vicinity of some sacred site. About 300 are to be found within a few miles of Stonehenge, and many groups lie along the line of the Dorset Cursus. At Winterbourne Stoke in Wiltshire a line of round barrows follows the axis of a large long barrow, pointing north-east, with a second line parallel to it. Indications of planned siting appear in almost every barrow cemetery, the growth

46

of which could have taken hundreds of years.

In many of these barrow cemeteries there are examples both of inhumation and cremation. Much care was lavished on the bodies of dead chieftains and their families. If inhumed, the corpse was usually placed, fully clothed and in a crouching position in a small pit at or near the centre of the area where the burial mound was to be thrown up; if cremation had taken place the bones were put in an urn or jar, and articles used during the dead person's lifetime were buried with the remains—battleaxes, knives, spearheads, flint arrowheads, dagger blades and other weapons of war and tools. The burials of women were accompanied with appropriate articles of ornament or domestic use such as bone needles, pins, small pots, necklaces, beads of shale and amber. A burial was first covered with turfs if available and then with material thrown up out of the surrounding ditch as it was dug. In some places round barrows were given stone revetments to help prevent the earth slipping. Finally a layer of chalk completed the process, and the barrow would remain for years, a brilliant white dot on the landscape. Even where chalk was unobtainable as in parts of Yorkshire, the process was often carried out in other substances. At Thornborough in North Yorkshire, excavations have shown that the banks surrounding the three circular henge monuments had been given a covering of gypsum to make them stand out from the rest of the landscape.

During the Bronze Age the construction of henges and other sacred sites continued. Elaborate additions were made to Stonehenge. At some time during this period 80 blue stones were brought from the Prescelly Mountains in South Wales and set up on the site. At a later date they were removed and the great blocks of sarsen were dragged from the Marlborough Downs, trimmed and set up as a circle of trilithons. Before the end of the Bronze Age this great structure, unequalled anywhere else in Europe, was complete. We still marvel at the ingenuity and labour involved in bringing these large stones such long distances and in setting them up.

The largest and most numerous Bronze Age monuments are to be found in Dorset and Wiltshire. Dorset has 1800 round barrows and Wiltshire 2200 besides the greatest artificial mound at Silbury Hill near Avebury. This enormous mound which even today contains $12\frac{1}{2}$ million cubic ft (35,394 cu.m), mainly of chalk, has been the focus of folklore and superstition for ages, and has defied all attempts so far to discover its purpose. We can only guess at the elaborate and prolonged ceremonies that must have taken place at some of these sites.

Elsewhere in England the henge monument was for the most part reduced to a single circle of standing stones with no ditch but often with an extra stone set near its centre or somewhere outside its circumference. These, large and small, may be found in various counties, especially Cornwall, Shropshire, East Yorkshire and Scotland, even as far north as the Orkneys where there are good examples at Stenness and Brogar. Many stone circles are too insignificant even to be mentioned in official lists of prehistoric monuments, though some of them have given rise to place-names, as at Ringstone Edge on the moors above Ripponden in West Yorkshire.

One of the most puzzling features of the late Neolithic and Bronze Ages is the so-called cup and ring marked stone. Rocks with markings of various kinds have been found in at least one neolithic passage grave in North Wales, while in a large region extending from Yorkshire to the Shetlands rocks have been found with hollows (cups) carved on them, sometimes surrounded by concentric circles (rings) and joined by wavy lines. What their object was, nobody has been able to say, but they probably had some religious significance.

Bronze Age rock carvings, Doddington, Northumberland

The division of history into so-called 'ages' is more a matter of convenience than a reality, for who can tell when a certain age began or when it ended? Even over these lengthy periods of prehistory there was a constant movement of peoples, and constant changes going on in ways of living. We know, for instance, that colder climatic conditions together with the incursions of bronze-using people from the Continent some 800 years before Christ helped to bring about a change from nomadic ways of life to the setting up of permanent homesteads. The use of the ox-drawn plough instead of the hoe led to the creation of small regularly shaped rectangular plots of land divided from others by banks or scarps made partly by man, partly by the washing down of earth on to a field and its levelling by the plough. These divisions or lynchets were often supported by low stone walls. The fields they marked out, misleadingly called 'Celtic' fields, appear in many parts of western England, and archaeologists have found near them traces of farmsteads. This kind of field, which existed well into Roman times, is difficult to see on ground level except from vantage-points when the sun is low, but may have been discovered by air reconnaissance.

THE IRON AGE

Gradually, round about the middle of the first millennium BC (c.500) the use of iron spread into Britain. There was nothing sudden about the change. In some cases iron or iron-style tools were acquired by people already settled here; in others they were brought by immigrants known today as Celts, who landed on the shores of Britain in the last stage of their movement westwards across Europe.

The effect of these migrations was felt at first in the South. Land-hunger brought wars; native tribes constructed hill-forts to help defend themselves, and these hill-forts, which in time appeared all over Britain, are one of the main features of the Iron Age. New dangers created closer social organization into larger units. Tribes became concentrated under warlike chieftains, often leaders of armed bands who set themselves up in these forts. War and raiding became

Lynchets, Gordale Bridge, West Yorkshire

a way of life. Religious monuments such as the henge and stone circle were no longer either created or respected, and no more burial mounds were thrown up, for even the later Bronze Age peoples had given up building round barrows and, after cremating their dead, had buried them in cemeteries known as urn-fields. Thus farming and fighting went on at the same time and archaeology has given us ample evidences of both.

A hill-fort is a fortified enclosure on a hilltop or ridge, constructed so as to take advantage of natural features for defence against marauders or invaders. Many, as the name indicates, were on the summits of hills, commanding extensive views over the surrounding countryside. Others were on ridges, protected on two or three sides by steep natural slopes and on the more vulnerable sides by single or multiple banks and ditches. Promontory forts were constructed where spits of high land dominated plains or valleys, and cliff forts were made to turn headlands such as Flamborough (Humberside), Treryn Dinas (Cornwall) and Hengistbury Head (Hampshire) into strongholds.

Their uses varied considerably as did the areas they enclosed. Earlier and smaller ones may have been temporary places of refuge in times of danger but left unoccupied in peace time; others may have been the headquarters of petty chieftains with their families and private armies.

The last half of the first millennium BC was a period of continual movement when the country was gradually overrun by Celtic peoples who in turn created their own hill-forts with varied uses and with more ingenious methods of defence. In size these vary from no more than an acre to an area large enough to accommodate a whole tribe.

Bagendon (Gloucestershire) enclosed 200 acres (81 ha). Stanwick (North Yorkshire), constructed in the 1st century AD and enlarged on two separate

Ramparts of Maiden Castle, Dorset

occasions, was at its greatest extent a tribal stronghold covering 747 acres (302 ha). In fact, every notable hill-fort has its own characteristics and merits separate study. Ramparts were timber-laced or dry-walled and some had internal walks. Ditches varied in number, width and distance one from another and from the main fortifications. Entrances were of many ingenious designs, some false to trap attackers, some turned inwards to force them to run a gauntlet of fire; others were staggered so that the true entrance did not appear opposite a gap in the external rampart, while others had enclosures with massive outer earthworks outside their gates to foil direct attacks. Many of these hill-forts must have been almost impossible to take by direct assault. In some forts, especially in Scotland, the stones of their timber-laced walls or ramparts have been fused and 'vitrified' by extreme heat. It is thought that this may have been caused by the timber ties, probably dried out by age, catching fire, and the resulting spaces acting as flues. This could have been the result either of accident or attack by an enemy.

Where hill-forts were not constructed, other natural

defences were made use of. In Norfolk there were lowland fortifications where marsh and river offered means of defence. In various parts of Scotland fortified towers or brochs were set up. Near some of these forts may be found traces of 'Celtic' fields, while in and around most have been unearthed all manner of articles of war, farming and domestic use.

The inhabitants of some Iron Age village settlements in Cornwall dug out underground shelters, roofed them over and may have used them either as storage chambers or refuges. A similar development occurred in Scotland where 'earth-houses' or souterrains are found, probably going back to the Bronze Age.

THE ROMAN PERIOD

The movement of peoples was still going on in Britain during Roman times. Julius Caesar destroyed one of the British tribal capitals in 54 BC. By AD 43 when the Claudian invasion took place the country was already divided into territories occupied by various tribes. The bones of young warriors found in the ditches of some Iron Age hill-forts bear testimony to the ferocity of the resistance against Roman arms. Thus, foreign manners and customs were suddenly thrust on a civilization which was and which remained, even during the Roman occupation, Iron Age in character but using articles such as pots and metalware coming from other parts of the Roman Empire.

Once the land had been conquered, the hill-forts were no longer used as native strongholds. In one or two cases, parts of them were re-fortified and turned into Roman fortlets. After the rebellions of the Iceni and the Brigantes had been crushed, a long period of peace began in which the tribes settled down to their agricultural pursuits and the country was opened up by the making of roads. British tribal capitals were sited in new Roman-style towns, as at Cirencester which supplanted Bagendon as capital of the Dobunni, and

Colchester which became a Roman town in place of the neighbouring lowland settlement of the Catuvellauni.

The conquest of Britain was as methodical as that of any other country either before or since. The Iron Age forts of Wessex and the Severn valley fell in quick succession, and legionary forts were set up at Gloucester (Glevum), Wroxeter (Viroconium) and Lincoln (Lindum). To hold land already conquered and to speed up the conquest of the rest, these military posts had to be connected with Roman bases in the south-east and with each other by an efficient road system, the first ever constructed in Britain. Westwards from London a road ran to Silchester and thence to Gloucester. Later, as the Second Legion was moved to Caerleon, the road was extended and became the supply route for the conquest of South Wales. Watling Street, running through the Midlands, connected London with Wroxeter and from it a road later ran to Chester which eventually became a legionary fortress. Thus bases were set up for the conquest of North Wales and the north-west of what is now England. Ermine Street, running due north from London, was the way to Lincoln and subsequently to Hadrian's Wall. These three highways were connected during the early years of the conquest by another, now known as the Fosse Way, which ran south-west from Lincoln, crossing all three. On this skeleton of highways the whole of the later Roman road system was constructed. It was extended by a road running westwards from Silchester to Bath (Aquae Sulis) and thence to the south-west, and by two others running west and east of the Pennines northwards to the posts on Hadrian's Wall and into what is now Scotland. Thus it became possible to move troops and supplies speedily from one part of the country to another. After the end of the revolts, York became the springboard for the complete subjugation of the North. The two legions based on Gloucester also pushed forward and set up new legionary fortresses at Caerleon in south Wales and Chester respectively.

The main factor, both in the exploitation of British resources and the defence of the country was the new road system. To the Romans a road was not merely a way from one place to another; it was as much a creation of the builder and engineer as a public building, a fort or a dock. It was created out of materials, stone, pebbles, clay, flint etc. which happened to be available locally, and it ran in as direct a course as possible through cuttings, along the sides of hills, across valleys, to its ultimate destination. Many of these roads, marked Roman Road on the Ordnance Survey maps of today, are still in use; others have left traces in all parts, across open country, and can still be traversed for long distances on foot.

The original intention of Rome was to conquer the whole island, and in AD 83 the Commander Julius Agricola moved with a powerful force into Scotland. By AD 80 he had established the Forth–Clyde frontier; in 81 roads and forts were built in south Scotland and

Roman road, Wheeldale Moor

in 83 he took an army north, completely defeating the native tribes at the battle of Mons Graupius near the sea in north-east Scotland, the exact site of which has never been found. Forts were placed at the entrances of the main valleys leading into the Highlands and a legionary fortress was set up at Inchtuthil. These forts were, however, abandoned shortly after the recall of Agricola in the same year as his victory, and the Romans never succeeded in consolidating their hold on the Highlands.

Instead the Emperor Hadrian decided on the building of a wall connecting the forts between the Tyne and the Solway. Thus Hadrian's Wall became the visible frontier of the Roman Empire, though there were Roman garrisons at various key points outside it to guard the approaches. Twenty years later the Emperor Antoninus Pius advanced the frontier to the Forth–Clyde line by the building of the Antonine Wall but, owing to pressure from tribes in the north, it was abandoned, and the end of the century saw the rebuilding of Hadrian's Wall by the Roman Emperor Severus. For almost two more centuries, though breached in 296 and again in 367, the Wall remained, as Hadrian had designed it to be, a frontier separating the barbarians from the Romans. It was supported and supplied by an elaborate system of forts, and by roads running both east and west of the Pennines. Visible remains both of the Wall and some of these forts are open to the visitor. The Antonine Wall, built mainly of turf or clay, and for the greater part of the Roman period lying outside the permanent frontier, has been by no means so well preserved, but in places its forts and parts of the ramparts may still be seen.

To ensure the defence of the country, northern England was turned into one great military establishment backed by the two legionary fortresses of Chester and York. At points on the roads running to the frontier stood posting stations and forts; on open land within easy reach of these roads there still remain traces of practice camps, marching camps and signal stations, while at Corbridge, on the spot where Dere Street, the main road to the north, crossed the Stanegate running east—west, a great arsenal and supply depot was established. Outside the military depot a busy little town covering some 40 acres (16.2 ha) grew up. Here, buildings belonging to the supply base and military arsenal are open to view.

Protected by the Wall and the forts, the rest of Britain enjoyed a period of peace probably unequalled in duration since the beginning of the Bronze Age. New tribal capitals developed into Roman-style towns, each with its forum, basilica, public baths and temples. Some of these, such as Silchester, have completely disappeared and are now under the plough; others lie beneath more modern urban development and visible remains are few. The roads leading to these busy commercial and administrative centres must have been alive with traffic, and excavation has revealed street plans, house plans and many articles of daily use which give us an insight into the lives of the people of those days. Outside the town walls are the remains of amphitheatres and cemeteries.

In the countryside two civilizations, the Roman and the Celtic, existed at the same time. In places remote from centres of civilization, such as Anglesey and West Cornwall, there were native villages where the inhabitants lived very much as their forbears had done in walled hut settlements. On the downlands the so-called 'Celtic' fields were still being cultivated. In other parts of England, notably Herefordshire and Yorkshire, caves which had been inhabited by men in palaeolithic times were still being used as shelters. Even there, among the remains have been found articles manufactured and imported from the Continent.

Nearer the centres of civilization, Celtic and Roman ways of life mingled. A British native farmer, prominent in his tribe might easily become a tribal official, a magistrate or even a senator under Roman rule. Contact with Roman ways of life influenced him profoundly. In place of his native hut, he might establish himself in a villa, have his sons educated to speak Latin and adopt Roman ways, and thus the new civilization spread among the tribal aristocracy.

There were some hundreds of Roman or Romano-British villas, especially in the south and south-east of the country. Each one housed a self-contained and self-sufficing community, providing all the necessities of life—food, clothing and shelter from its own estate, employing slaves as farm labourers, craftsmen, household servants and clerks, relying on the outside world mainly for the extras and luxuries of life which were obtained through the trading of surplus produce.

The plans of these villas vary considerably. Some were simply rooms connected by a passage, others had verandas or corridors running along the front of the building, others were built round courtyards or even had extra wings built out. The greater number were furnished with central heating by means of the hypocaust, a system of flues running under floors and in the walls of rooms, heated by an external underground furnace. Some had bath suites as elaborate as the baths in the towns, and several useful and ornamental features—fountains, mosaic floors, tessellated pavements, gardens, clerestory windows lighting rooms from above, ornamental wells and springs. They were very pleasant places in which the Romano-British landowners could live.

In various parts of the country, the remains of Roman temples have been found. Shortly after the conquest by Claudius (AD 43) a great temple was built in the classical style on top of the hill at Colchester for the worship of the deified Emperor. It was a rectangular building set within a large courtyard, and it stood on a platform or podium founded on two massive con-

*'Spring',
Chedworth
Roman villa
mosaic,
Gloucestershire*

crete vaults. It was destroyed in the revolt of Queen
Boudicca in AD 60. Many centuries later a Norman
castle was erected on its foundations and can still be
visited. Temples of a similar design were at Wroxeter
and Lydney (Gloucestershire) and a smaller one at
Caerwent.

A much commoner type of temple was the shrine
surrounded on all sides by a columned portico or
veranda. These shrines are believed to be of Celtic
origin. Traces have been found by excavation and air
photography. They varied in shape from the 16-sided
temple at Silchester to the simple square or rectangle
with an enclosed sanctuary in the centre, and were
usually surrounded by a courtyard or enclosed garden.

During the last years of the Empire the worship of
the god Mithras became popular, especially in ruling
and military circles, and small mithraic temples have
been discovered at Carrawborough on Hadrian's Wall
and in Walbrook, London, among other places.

One of the first things to be seen on approaching a Roman town would be the cemetery. Until Christian times the Romans were accustomed to cremate their dead and to bury the remains outside the walls in burial grounds usually situated near the side of a high road. Over the tombs they raised monuments and placed slabs of stone on which were inscribed the names and ranks of the dead, together with short recitals of their virtues. Many of these have been recovered and may be seen in museums.

Some wealthy Britons did not, however, entirely give up the old Iron Age custom of erecting barrows over their cremated dead, and placing plentiful assortments of grave-goods with the bones. Roman barrows are to be found mainly in the south and east of England in land occupied by the Belgic tribes. Four of the largest are the Bartlow Hills in north Essex. There are others in Kent, Hertfordshire, Dorset, Wiltshire and as far north as Lincolnshire.

In the late 3rd century AD, two new threats to the Roman peace appeared in Britain. The first came when Saxon raiders from outside the Roman Empire descended on the coasts of Britain year after year, plundering and burning villas, towns and villages. The second was in the year 286 when a usurper named Carausius, who had been put in command of forces to deal with these pirates proclaimed himself an independent ruler. He governed Britain and part of northern Gaul for seven years until one of the Roman Emperors named Constantius advanced on him and captured the town of Boulogne (Gessoriacum). Soon after this Carausius was murdered and Constantine invaded Britain and restored order.

During this period a string of forts known as the Forts of the Saxon Shore were built at Brancaster, Burgh Castle (Norfolk), Bradwell (Essex), Reculver, Richborough, Dover, Lympne (Kent), Pevensey (East Sussex) and Portchester (Hampshire). They may possibly have been built by Carausius as some authorities suggest, to protect himself either from a Roman invasion or Saxon raids, but they were certainly strengthened by Constantius and supplemented by signal stations elsewhere on the coasts to give warning of the approach of enemies.

At the beginning of the 5th century the time came when the Roman Empire, already threatened by barbarian invaders, could no longer afford to defend Britain against Pict and Saxon. In AD 410 the Goths under their leader Alaric entered and sacked Rome itself. In the same year the Roman legions were withdrawn from Britain and the people were left to fend for themselves. The Wall had been breached in the north, the Forts of the Saxon Shore fell to ruin, the Roman towns gradually decayed and, just as had happened many times in former ages, a new race with new ways of life and a different language, colonized the island.

Remains of Roman temple, Chester

GAZETTEER

Aconbury Iron Age hill-fort *Hereford and Worcester, 4½ miles (7.2 km) S of Hereford* Constructed at some time in the 1st century BC, this hill-fort follows the contours along the sides of fairly steep slopes. Enclosing 17 ac (7 ha), it was defended by one bank and ditch with a counterscarp bank. The entrance on the SE was turned inwards. The fort was occupied until after the Roman conquest.

Almondbury Iron Age hill-fort *West Yorks, 1¾ miles (2.8 km) SE of Huddersfield town centre, on Castle Hill* The western half of these fortifications was destroyed when a castle was erected there in the reign of Stephen (1135–54) and only traces of the fort still remain. The first small fort was built in the 3rd century BC on the SW of the summit, with an in-turned entrance facing NE and a single bank and ditch. Later it was extended to enclose the whole summit with an in-turned entrance on the NE, defended by a rampart, ditch and bank with more banks lower down the slope. The main rampart was later strengthened by timber lacing, and new banks and ditches constructed.

It is thought probable that Cartimandua, the pro-Roman queen of the Brigantes, had her headquarters here (AD 69) while her husband, King Venutius, re-sisted them at Stanwick in north Yorkshire. The fort was systematically destroyed by the Romans.

Ambresbury Banks Iron Age hill-fort *Essex, 1¾ miles (2.8 km) S of Epping* This rectangular 11½-ac (4.5-ha) camp is surrounded by woodland. Built approximately 100 BC, it was defended by a single ditch and bank with a probable entrance on the W side.

In the same area is **Loughton Camp**, ¾ m (1.2 km)

NNW of Loughton, enclosing some 6½ ac (2.6 ha) defended by a bank and ditch with steep slopes on the W side.

Popular legend has connected these two camps with the revolt and defeat of Boudicca (AD 60) but any association with this event is unlikely.

ANGLESEY *Gwynedd*

Neolithic peoples arriving by sea colonized Anglesey in the 3rd millennium BC. At that time the interior of the island was heavily wooded, and prehistoric man was compelled to make his settlements on the light soils near the coast.

At least 54 neolithic burial chambers are known to have existed on Anglesey. Of these about 20 still remain, 8 being in the guardianship of the Department of the Environment. The discovery of beakers in the neolithic tomb chambers goes to show that Bronze Age peoples were probably assimilated into the original population, and the 30 standing stones which remain may have been fragments of stone circles. During this age men were more able to penetrate into the central areas of the island, and the remains of some 20 round barrows are to be found there.

The Celtic occupation of Anglesey has been proved by the discovery of numerous articles, mainly for use in war, at Llyn Cerrig Bach opposite the southern tip of Holyhead Island. Some of these were imported.

In AD 78 North Wales was conquered by Agricola and the country was controlled by a Roman fort set up at Segontium (Caernarvon). Anglesey, being off the main lines of communication, then consisted mainly of open villages which, during the later Empire, came to be walled owing to the attacks of seaborne raiders. Some had banks and ditches, while in one, Caer Gybi dating from the 3rd or 4th century AD, were works of a more advanced nature, its walls and towers revealing Roman influence.

Anglesey and Caernarvon were among the first parts of Britain to be neglected by Rome when internal pressure placed greater demands on her armed forces. Segontium was finally abandoned in about AD 385.

Barclodiad y gawres neolithic passage grave (DE) *on the coast 2 miles (3.2 km) N of Aberffraw* The original mound, 80 ft (24 m) in diameter, had within it a passage leading S into a chamber from which smaller chambers ran SE and W. In the western chamber the cremated bones of two persons were found. Five of the stones which line the passage and chambers contain designs of spirals, chevrons, zigzags and lozenges, designs only seen on one other neolithic tomb in Britain, also in Anglesey. The chamber has been put in order and measures have been taken to protect the inscriptions on the stones.

Bodowyr neolithic burial chamber *1¾ miles (2.8 km) NW of the new parish church, Llanidan* Of this chamber which resembles the Cornish quoits, only three uprights and the great capstone still remain

Bodowyr burial chamber, Anglesey

in position. A fourth upright is too short to reach the capstone, and on the SW side of the chamber two other stones lie partly buried.

Bryn Celli ddu neolithic passage grave (DE)
1 mile (1.6 km) E of Llanidan Fab church This is one of the rare examples of a passage grave under a circular mound, originally 160 ft (48.8 m) in diameter, but now little more than half that. The polygonal chamber almost at the centre of the mound is entered from a forecourt by means of a passage. The mound is ringed by a circle of large stones which at one time were buried under it.

Bryn Celli ddu contained the only other stone in Britain besides Barclodiad y gawres on which were neolithic designs. This is now in the National Museum of Wales at Cardiff and a plaster cast has been put in its place.

Some skeletons were found when the chamber was opened many years ago and the remains of fires and an ox burial were discovered in the forecourt.

Bryn Celli ddu passage grave, Anglesey

Caer Gybi Roman fort see ROMAN FORTS, page 137.

Caer Leb earthwork *1½ miles (2.4 km) NW of Llanidan old church* The enclosure was probably made during the latter years of the Roman Empire. It is 5-sided, defended by two banks and ditches of which the outer ones on the NE and SE have disappeared, the material from them having been used to fill the ditches.

Caer y twyr Iron Age hill-fort *1¾ miles (2.8 km) W of Holyhead on the summit of the mountain* The area, 17 ac (6.9 ha) in extent, is protected by steep slopes on all sides, a rampart with an in-turned entrance at the NE corner, but no ditch. The best preserved portion of the rampart is on the N where it reached a maximum height of 10 ft (3 m) with, in places, the remains of a rampart walk. Natural slopes made it one of the best defensive points on the island.

Castell Bryn Gwyn defensive site *1½ miles (2.4 km) WSW of Llanidan new parish church* The rampart and ditch defending the original neolithic camp were remodelled during Roman times. There was an entrance on the SW which was blocked when the rampart was doubled in width and a new entrance was made, probably on the N side. The final fortifications were added in the shape of a deep surrounding ditch and a rampart revetted with timber, added about AD 50. Pottery of neolithic and early Roman times has been found on the site.

Din Lligwy walled homestead (DE) *1 mile (1.6 km) E of Penrhos Lligwy church* At some time during the last years of the Roman occupation this native village was fortified, probably by a local chieftain, and used as a residence. The buildings within it, five rectangular and two circular, all built out of massive stone blocks, stand within a five-sided enclosure, the remains of whose protecting wall are from 4 to 5 ft (1.2 to 1.5 m) thick. The entrance on the NE leads through a rectangular enclosure into the main area.

There is no evidence that this outstanding site was lived in after about AD 400.

Holyhead Mountain hut circles *2¼ miles (3.6 km) W of Holyhead on the SW slope of Holyhead Mountain* In 1865 there were at least 50 huts on this slope and probably more before that time. Only 20 now remain, some circular, some rectangular.

The roofs of the huts were probably turf-thatched and supported by central upright poles. Some have hearth-places and slabs making beds and seats. They were inhabited during Iron Age and Roman times.

Lligwy neolithic burial chamber (DE) *1¼ miles (2 km) E of Penrhos Lligwy church* The huge capstone of this remarkable monument is 18 ft (5.5 m) in length and of such a weight that two-thirds of the supports are now broken or underground, leaving only a low space beneath it. When excavated, the remains of 30 persons were discovered together with animal bones and pottery.

Penrhos-Feilw standing stones *1¾ miles (2.8 km) SW of Holyhead* The stones are 11 ft (3.3 m) apart and stand 10 ft (3 m) high. There is a tradition that they were once the centre of a Bronze Age stone circle and that between them was found a stone cist containing human remains and stone weapons, but this cannot be proved.

1 mile (1.6 km) SE of Holyhead is the single standing stone of **Ty Mawr,** 9 ft (2.7 m) high.

Trefignath neolithic burial chamber (DE) *1½ miles (2.4 km) SE of Holyhead* Very little trace of the mound once covering this chamber now exists. The original passage was formed of large flanking stones covered by two capstones, one overlapping the other. The passage was divided into three or four separate chambers by large cross-slabs. Of these the most easterly may still be seen, its two portals standing to a height of 7 ft (2.1 m).

THE ANTONINE WALL (DE)

In AD 122 the Emperor Hadrian established the frontier of the Roman Empire in Britain by building his wall from the Solway to the Tyne. He was succeeded in AD 138 by Antoninus Pius who decided to advance this frontier, reoccupying southern Scotland and building another wall from the Forth to the Clyde.

In the years 142–3 this wall, a long rampart of turf blocks with a ditch in front of it, was erected on a stone foundation from 14 to 16 ft (4.25 to 4.9 m). Though the Wall was not as much of an obstacle as that of Hadrian, the ditch, some 40 ft (12.1 m) wide and 12 ft (3.7 m) deep, was probably more so. Forts were erected all along its line at intervals of about 2 miles (3.2 km), attached to the rear of the rampart and linked by a military road. The plans of many of these forts are known as a result of excavation. The wall was twice attacked and many forts destroyed. Before the end of the century it had been abandoned.

Most of the visible remains of the Wall and its

Antonine Wall at Falkirk (parallel to main road)

additional works are to be found in the neighbourhood of **Rough Castle (DE)** $2\frac{1}{2}$ miles (4 km) W of Falkirk best reached by a lane from Bonnybridge. The fort was defended by a ditch 40 ft (12.1 m) wide. To the north of the ditch a number of pits in line, now known as 'the lilies', served as an additional defence. The Military Way ran W to E through the fort and through a fortified enclosure to the E of it. Foundations of some of the administrative buildings have been excavated.

Near Rough Castle the following may be seen:

At **Bonnyside East**, $\frac{1}{4}$ mile (0.4 km) W of Rough Castle, N of the lane to Bonnybridge, a semicircular mound which when excavated in 1957 was found to have a stone base with a possible turf platform. Remains of charred wood suggest that it was a signalling post.

At **Seabegs Wood**, 1 mile (1.6 km) SW of Bonnybridge on S side of the B816, $\frac{1}{4}$ mile (0.4 km) of the Wall with ditch 40 ft (12.1 m) wide and outer mound. The line of the Military Way may still be seen about 16 ft wide (4.9 m), 50 to 150 yd (45.7 to 127 m) S of the Wall.

At **Tentfield East**, 2 miles (3.2 km) W of Falkirk on the B816 road, halfway between Watling Lodge and Tentfield Plantation, another semicircular mound, probably the remains of a beacon stance.

At **Watling Lodge** on B816, $\frac{1}{4}$-mile (0.4-km) length of ditch 40 ft (12.1 m) wide borders the road.

In two other places, remains of the Wall and its ancillary works are to be seen:

At **Croy Hill**, $1\frac{1}{4}$ miles (2.1 km) SE of Kilsyth, just E of Croy, a section of the Wall and the 40-ft (12.2-m) wide rock-cut ditch.

At **Kilpatrick Cemetery, Bearsden**, two exposed stretches of the foundations 15 ft (4.6 m) wide, showing drainage culverts and terracing on the hill slope.

Arbor Low, Bronze Age sacred site and round barrow (DE) *Derbyshire, 5 miles (8 km) SW of Bakewell* This henge monument was probably erected about 2000–1600 BC, and includes a circle of standing stones, now fallen and in fragments. In the centre are the remains of a U-shaped cove. The stone circle is surrounded by a rock-cut ditch with a limestone bank 250 ft (76.5 m) in diameter and there are entrances on the N and S sides.

Adjoining the bank on the E side of the S entrance is a round bronze age barrow 7 ft (2.1 m) high, in which were found a bone pin, a flint strike-a-light and two food vessels placed in a stone cist.

Ardestie Iron Age souterrain (DE) *Tayside, on N side of main Perth-Arbroath road before reaching Ardestie cross-roads* Although the end and the roof of the souterrain are absent, this 76 ft (23.2 m) long example is one of the best.

The floor is rough-paved and a drain runs down the middle under the paving. On the site are also the

Arbor Low, Derbyshire

Avebury, Wiltshire, showing outer stone circle

remains of four huts of which the largest has a cup and ring stone built into the wall.

Arthur's Stone neolithic chambered long barrow (DE) *Hereford and Worcester, 1 mile (1.6 km) N of Dorstone* This chambered tomb was once covered by a large mound orientated N–S. The huge capstone remains, supported by nine uprights. North of the burial chamber was an antechamber connected with it by an approach passage. The two isolated stones S of the barrow may have been part of the system of stones erected round it.

AVEBURY AND NEIGHBOURING SITES *Wiltshire*
The great stone circle at Avebury (owned by **NT** guardianship of **DE**) 1140 ft (347 m) in diameter with its surrounding earthwork is one of the most remarkable monuments of neolithic times. The earthwork, a circular bank of chalk, once white, but now overgrown with grass, encloses first a ditch, originally

30 ft (9.1 m) deep and 70 ft (21.3 m) wide, and within it is the roughly circular plateau round the edge of which stood the great stone circle of more than 100 sarsen stones, 27 of these still standing. Within this were two smaller stone circles, each roughly 330 ft (100 m) in diameter and having about 30 uprights. Only four stones remain of the more northerly of these two, and at its centre was a U-shaped cove consisting of three large stones, two of which still stand. The southern circle has five surviving stones. Parts of both these circles are under modern buildings.

There were four entrances, through which roads now run, and from the southern one a double row of standing stones now known as Kennet Avenue connected Avebury with **The Sanctuary on Overton Hill (DE)** $1\frac{1}{2}$ miles (2.4 km) to the SE, passing the village of West Kennet. At the northern part of the Avenue the positions where stones once stood have been marked, but elsewhere very few are to be seen. The Sanctuary, lying near West Kennet, had four concentric rings of wooden posts surrounded by two concentric rings of stones. It was discovered by aerial photography in 1930, having been destroyed in the 18th century. Originally it appears to have been a wooden building set up by neolithic peoples, subsequently extended and finally replaced by the Beaker people with two rings of sarsens. Concrete blocks now mark the positions. Both Avebury and the Sanctuary reached their final form during the late Neolithic Age (about 2000 BC).

The area within 2 miles (3.2 km) of Avebury is dotted with prehistoric remains—stone circles, long and round barrows and standing stones. Among the best known are:

The West Kennet Long Barrow, one of the largest and most magnificent neolithic chambered tombs in Britain, its chalk mound roughly 330 ft (100.6 m) long and 8 ft (2.4 m) high. The burial chamber occu-

(upper) *Exterior of West Kennet long barrow, Wiltshire*
(lower) *Interior of West Kennet*

pies only one end of the earthwork, and consists of a small forecourt and entrance passage with five chambers opening from it. These are built of large sarsens and roofed with flat capstones. The original entrance is now blocked by another large sarsen. In the various chambers the remains of 46 persons were discovered.

North of the road from West Kennet to Beckhampton stands **Silbury Hill (DE)**, the largest prehistoric artificial mound in Europe. The fact that the Roman road to Bath makes a detour round it dates it before the Roman occupation. It probably began its existence as a small mound during neolithic times, later capped with chalk and extended. The discovery of sarsens at its centre suggests that it may have been a round barrow but there is no record of any burial having been found in it.

Farther along the Bath road, $\frac{1}{4}$ mile (0.4 m) NE of Beckhampton, are two stones known as the **Long Stones**, named Adam and Eve. These may have been part of a ceremonial avenue or of a cove. When Adam fell in 1911 a male skeleton and a beaker were dis-

Silbury Hill, Wiltshire

covered, having been buried at its foot.

Two miles (3.2 km) NW of Avebury is the neolithic causewayed camp of **Windmill Hill (NT).** It was made round about 2500 BC by the digging of three concentric ditches on the hill slopes, enclosing some 21 acres (8.5 ha) and interrupted by a number of entrance gaps or causeways. The numerous finds from this site, especially household goods and pottery moulded by hand, dark in colour, round-bottomed and decorated with marks on shoulder and rim, have given the name Windmill Hill culture to people who practised similar domestic arts. (See Front Endpaper.)

Badbury Rings Iron Age hill-fort *Dorset, 3½ miles (5.6 km) W of Wimborne Minster* This banked and ditched fort on the wooded summit of a hill is a well-known landmark. It had two banks and ditches with a third, the outermost, added some time after its construction. There are entrances E and W, the former staggered and the latter with outworks added.

The importance of this earthwork continued into Roman times. It stands near the meeting-place of two Roman roads, the Ackling Dyke (Old Sarum to Dorchester) and the road from Bath to Poole Harbour.

Bagendon Iron Age hill-fort *Gloucestershire, 2½ miles (4 km) NW of Cirencester* This important fort whose earthworks enclose 200 acres (81 ha) was the tribal centre of the Dobunni. It was constructed, probably about AD 15 when the tribe was allied with the Catuvellauni of the SE. Through this alliance the settlement enjoyed a brief period of great prosperity. Continental glazed pottery, brooches and articles of bronze and iron were imported, and the Dobunni struck their own coins.

The fort was defended on three sides by ditches; on the N side a 10-ft (3-m) high bank at Scrubditch,

Badbury Rings, Dorset

and other banks and ditches on the S and E sides.

When the Romans invaded Britain in AD 43 the allegiance of the Dobunni was divided, the northern part of the tribe around Bagendon surrendering themselves, the southern part resisting. The Romans finally reduced the whole Severn valley, the people of Bagendon receiving more lenient treatment than others, but they were later moved *en masse* to the new Roman tribal capital of Cirencester.

Barbury Castle Iron Age hill-fort *Wiltshire, 2½ m (4 km) S of Wroughton* Situated on the edge of the Marlborough Downs, this fort in open country is ideal for exploration. In a strong position, its 11½ acres (4.7 ha), oval in shape, are defended by concentric banks and ditches. The entrances are E and W, and at the former the remains of additional defensive works may be seen. Below, on the hill-slope to the east are the 'Celtic' fields of Burderop Down, covering more than 140 acres (57 ha), one of the most outstanding groups of this type of field in England.

Belas Knap neolithic long barrow (DE) *Gloucester-shire, 1¾ miles (2.8 km) S of Winchcombe*   A very good example of a barrow with a false entrance and with entries to its chambers in the sides, reached by means of short passages. The barrow, more than 170 ft (51.8 m) long, is orientated N–S; it had a revetment, a false entrance and a forecourt with two horn-like extensions at the N end. This may have been designed either to ward off evil spirits or to fool possible tomb-robbers.

Two of the chamber entrances are let into the E side, one half-way along the W side and a fourth at the S end. The barrow had a revetment of stone all round it.

Bindon Hill Iron Age promontory fort *Dorset, S of West Lulworth*   The E part of the ridge on which this fort stands is a Ministry of Defence artillery range. It is unique in being a probable beach-head fortification made by Iron Age invaders (c 400 BC) who established themselves on the S coast, and was constructed to control Lulworth Cove.

Barbury Castle, Wiltshire

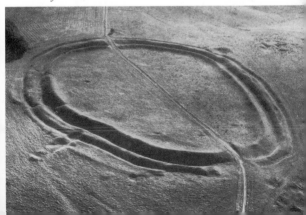

The rampart and ditch extend for 1½ miles (2.4 km) along the ridge, cutting off about 400 acres (162 ha). A N–S cross-dyke cuts off about 13 acres (5 ha) at the W end, the only portion that can be visited. This cross-bank was never completed.

Blackbury Castle Iron Age hill-fort (DE) *Devon, 3 miles (4.8 km) NW of Seaton* This small oval fort, enclosing some 4 acres (1.6 ha) has unusually well-preserved earthworks; a bank, in places 10 ft (3 m) high, and a well-marked ditch. The only original entrance was on the S side, turned slightly outwards, gated and probably bridged. It was given extra protection by a triangular barbican which remained unfinished. The fort is in a beech plantation and is clear of undergrowth.

Bredon Hill Iron Age promontory fort *Hereford and Worcester, 5 m (8 km) NE of Tewkesbury* At some time early in the 1st century BC immigrants

Bredon Hill, Hereford and Worcester

from the SW were attracted to the Severn valley by the prospect of iron deposits, and here, on a N-facing spur of Bredon Hill they built a fort, protected on two sides by a small bank and ditch with a staggered entrance. Later in that century the fort was extended to cover 22 acres (8.9 ha) by a second bank and ditch which still exist, entrances at the two ends providing access to the space between the two ramparts. The staggered entrance to the inner fort was strengthened.

Some years before the Roman invasion the fort was attacked and taken, probably by a Belgic tribe. More than 50 young male defenders had been killed at the main inner gate and their heads put up on poles. By the time the Romans reached this part of Britain the fort was deserted.

Bridestones chambered long barrow *Cheshire, 3 miles (4.8 km) E of Congleton* Here, on a slope of the Pennines 820 ft (219 m) above sea level, a group of neolithic peoples built a large E–W-facing burial mound about 300 ft (91.4 m) long, one of the largest in England. The mound has now almost disappeared, leaving the remains of a chambered tomb 18 ft (5.5 m) long, divided into two compartments by a stone which was originally holed in the centre. The forecourt was at the E end of the barrow, and traces of charcoal were discovered there, probably the remains of ancient funeral ceremonies.

THE BRISTOL IRON AGE HILL-FORTS *Avon*
Three of these forts, **Clifton Down**, **Borough Walls** and **Stokeleigh**, though separated by the Avon Gorge, are within ¼ mile (0.4 km) of each other, and probably contemporary (2nd–1st century BC). The triple banks and ditches of Clifton Down are well preserved on the N and enclose 3 acres (1.2 ha). Borough Walls camp had three banks and two ditches, but has now been almost obliterated by quarrying. Stokeleigh faces

Borough Walls across a valley. It is a 6-acre (2.4-ha) enclosure with two banks and ditches, with extra defences on the NW and a cliff on the NE. The site is easily accessible and the results of an excavation of part of a rampart still remain uncovered.

Blaise Castle, 1 mile (1.6 km) NW of Westbury-on-Trym, enclosing some 6 acres (2.4 ha), is probably earlier than the three above-mentioned (c 250 BC). The steep slopes on the S and E formed a natural defence, while double banks and ditches protected the N and W. A quarter of a mile (0.4 km) SW of this fort is the small 1-acre (0.4-ha) promontory fort of **Kings Weston,** situated on a long narrow hill, the steep slopes on N and E giving sufficient protection except for a bank and rock-cut ditch. Cutting off the spur of the hill 850 ft (261 m) to the W of the fort itself is another bank. Between this and the fort is a circular banked enclosure which may have contained a dwelling.

Broad Down Bronze Age barrow cemetery *Devon, 2¼ miles (3.6 km) S of Honiton*   Out of some 37 round bowl barrows in the 3 miles (4.8 km) between Gittisham Hill and Broad Down, about 24 are near enough together to be considered as a barrow cemetery. These mounds have yielded a great variety of grave goods and one cremation. Many have been robbed or defaced and some have been excavated.

BROCHS

The broch, which is unique to Scotland, is one of the most ingenious military works of prehistoric man. It was in essence a tall circular tower built of drystone blocks with a thick wall on ground level in which there was one opening or passage into which a stout door was let. Inside the enclosed area was a small courtyard with a central hearth round which timber lean-to constructions were arranged, supported at the rear by the inner wall of the broch. Either at ground floor or at first floor level the wall was hollow and it enclosed staircases and galleries, their stone-flagged floorings acting as bonds between inner and outer walls. Around the broch itself were fortifications consisting of ramparts, ditches and walls often enclosing other buildings. In Scotland, from Tayside southwards, only 11 remains of brochs have been found, but N and W of Inverness and on the Hebrides there are at least 50, on Orkney some 60 and on Shetland 50. In all, more than 500 are either known or suspected.

Edinshall (DE) *Borders, $2\frac{1}{4}$ miles (3.6 km) NW of Preston* One of the best preserved brochs of the Forth, it stands on the NW corner of an earlier hillfort and has walls 17 ft (5.2 m) thick. Within the thickness of the walls are five chambers including two guard cells at the entrances, and a staircase.

Scottish broch:
Carloway,
Lewis

Broch of Durness, Orkney

Tappoch *Central, 2¼ miles (3.6 km) NW of Larbert in Tor Wood* This is one of the best preserved brochs S of the Forth, with massive walls and an intact entrance passage. Pottery fragments, pieces of querns and slabs with cup and ring markings have been excavated here.

Torwoodlee fort and broch *Borders, 2 miles (3.2 km) NW of Galashiels* The pre-Roman fort was defended by two earthen ramparts, these now visible only on the N. The broch, at its W side, built later since its ditch cuts into that of the fort, has 18-ft (5.5-m) thick walls and there are cells within their thickness.

Excellent examples of brochs outside the sphere of Roman influence are to be found near Glenelg in the Highlands (outstanding examples **Dun Troddan** and **Dun Telve**) and **Dun Carloway** on the Island of Lewis. On Rousay Island (Orkney) is the broch of **Mid Howe**; on Mousa Island (Shetland) the **Broch of Mousa** and on the mainland of Shetland, near Lerwick, the oustanding broch of **Clickhimin**.

Bulstrode Camp Iron Age hill-fort (NT) *Gerrards Cross, Buckinghamshire* This site is worth more than casual inspection by the passer-by since it is so easily accessible, being on a public open space. The largest hill-fort in the county, its two ditches and ramparts still remain except on the W and NW. Of the three entrance gaps, it has not yet been found which is the original one.

The Bulwarks Iron Age earthworks *Minchinhampton Common, Gloucestershire, 2¾ miles (4.4 km) S of Stroud* It is suggested that this complex of earthworks may have been the headquarters of the British chieftain Caractacus when he rallied his followers for a last stand against the Romans in AD 49–50.

On all sides except the SE the site is defended by steep natural slopes, and here, a bank and rock-cut ditch more than a mile (1.6 km) long was cut in the spur of the hill, cutting off an area of 600 acres (242 ha), a space comparable with the other large Iron Age forts of Bagendon (Gloucestershire) and Stanwick (Yorkshire).

The bank was retained on its S side by a drystone wall, and Iron Age pottery recovered from the site proves that the works are of this period. There are also other banks and ditches of a later date, known as **Amberley Camp,** elsewhere on the Common.

Burrow Camp and Bury Ditches Iron Age hill-forts *Salop* These two hill-forts are situated within 4 miles (6.4 km) of each other between Hopesay and Clun. The former, covering 5 acres (2 ha), had four banks and ditches except on the NW where the steep slope made only one necessary. At an entrance on the S the ramparts were turned in; at another on the E the openings were staggered and the innermost bank in-turned.

Bury Ditches, overgrown with trees, had multiple

banks and ditches strengthening the steep surrounding slopes. On the NE where the ground is less steep there are five banks, and at the entrance here the innermost bank is in-turned. The SE entrance is given extra defence by the outer banks being turned outwards, the inner ones turned inwards, a rare method.

Buzbury Rings Iron Age hill-slope fort *Dorset, 2 miles (3.2 km) SE of Blandford* The B3082 Blandford-Wimborne road runs through the site. This fort is unique in not being on a promontory or a hill-top but on a slope, and with slight earthworks consisting of two banks and ditches enclosing in all some 12 acres (4.9 ha). Inside the outer bank is an extra ditch, also a unique feature. On the SW side there are sections of a third bank between the other two. There is a slightly in-turned entrance on the SW.

The situation of the fort, the defences and the traces of hut circles suggest that it was intended mainly for the herding of cattle, but that it could also be used for defensive purposes.

Caburn Iron Age hill-fort *East Sussex, 2 miles (3.2 km) E of Lewes* The site was probably occupied from about 300 BC to 100 BC with no fortifications whatever, and then round about the latter date the first bank and ditch were constructed, enclosing some $3\frac{1}{2}$ acres (1.4 ha). It was in the end probably taken by assault and then used as a store by the newcomers, the traces of many grain storage pits still remaining as depressions inside the ramparts.

At the time of the Roman conquest a new bank and ditch were constructed, and these remain. The bank was kept in place by timber revetting inside and out, and with timber tie-beams running through it.

Cadbury Castle hill-fort *Somerset, $\frac{1}{2}$ mile (0.8 km) SW of South Cadbury* This most important fort on

Cadbury Castle, Somerset

an isolated hill 400 ft (122 m) high was occupied by a neolithic farming community whose pottery and flints have been unearthed. A low bank then surrounded the 18-acre (7.3-ha) site.

During the Iron Age the fortifications were re-modelled and strengthened, the four complete rings of high banks and ditches being added. The original entrances were at the NE and SW. There were internal buildings including a smithy, a possible Celtic temple and houses.

Roman remains including equipment and a building suggest that the fort was taken and occupied by Roman soldiery for a time. The remains of 6th-century occupation by Romanized Britons connect the fort with the legends of King Arthur—the legendary Camelot.

Caer Caradoc Iron Age hill-fort *Salop, 1¾ miles (2.8 km) NE of Church Stretton* In spite of its altitude (1500 ft; 457 m) and the exposed position of this fort it appears to have been permanently occupied during the 2nd and 1st centuries BC. The 6 acres (2.4 ha) enclosed are defended by steep

85

natural slopes on all sides and by a bank of stone, possibly quarried from within the north end. There are extra defences round the N and S sides, and the only entrance, in-turned, is on the SE. It commands one of the most extensive views of any in Britain.

Cairnpapple Bronze Age henge and cairn (DE) *Lothian, 1¼ miles (2 km) ESE of Torphichen* This is one of the most interesting of the Bronze Age sites in SE Scotland. At about 2000 BC a small cremation cemetery was made here, consisting of seven small pits, in six of which human remains have been found. This was extended later by the erection of a henge with an outer ditch, surrounding a rock-cut grave marked by 10 stones and a large slab.

Between 1500 and 1000 BC the site was again used by people who placed a burial within the henge under a stone cist, accompanied by a food vessel. A mound or cairn was raised within the henge and stones were used to form a kerb to it. Later the cairn itself was extended to cover a much larger area and two urns containing cremated remains were buried in shallow pits at its edge.

Capel Garmon Neolithic chambered long barrow (DE) *Llanrwst, Gwynedd, 1 mile (1.6 km) S of Capel Garmon village* This tomb is set in a barrow 140 ft (42.7 m) long, with a single entrance at one side and a passage leading into the interior, then right and left into two burial chambers.

Neolithic pottery was found in the passage. At the eastern end of the barrow a drystone revetment wall forms two horns, like those of Belas Knap (Gloucestershire), enclosing a false entrance.

Car Dyke Roman canal *Cambridgeshire, linking the Cam at Waterbeach with the Old West River S of Haddenham* In the Fens the Romans were faced with two problems, transport and drainage. The Car Dyke, a flat-bottomed waterway 45 ft (13.7 m) wide at the surface, was designed to help solve both, making it possible to take corn by water from East Anglia to Lincoln, York and thence to the northern garrisons, and also to increase the surface area of water in the Fens and hasten evaporation. In its day it was probably a busy waterway, but now it is no more than a wide shallow overgrown ditch.

Carn Brea hill-fort and hut village *Cornwall, between Camborne and Redruth on the hill above Carnbrea village* Neolithic pottery and stone axes were discovered on this site. Later it was occupied by Iron Age people and was fortified with bank and ditch on the N, and two ramparts on the S where the land slopes less abruptly.

Within the 36 acres (14.6 ha) enclosed by the fort are traces of circular Iron Age huts. A medieval castle was built inside the enclosure. Near the monument at the W end was a gap, probably the original entrance.

Castle an Dinas Iron Age hill-fort *Cornwall, 2¼ miles (3.6 km) ESE of St Columb Major* Tin deposits exist near this massive hill-fort and it may have been associated with the industry. Its defences, consisting of three ramparts with a SW entrance, enclose an area of 6 acres (2.4 ha), the middle one being unfinished.

Castle How hill-fort *Cumbria, 5 miles (8 km) E of Cockermouth* Here, within easy reach of modern communications, is a fort, protected on the N and S by steep hill slopes, on the W by four ditches with counterscarp banks and on the E by two banks, ditches and counterscarp banks. These fortifications are all well defined, and this small but well-defended fort has a fine view over Bassenthwaite Lake. It was built by natives, probably during the Roman period.

Castle Law Iron Age hill-fort (DE) *Lothian, 3 miles (4.8 km) S of Fairmilehead* The palisade, the only defence round the original enclosure, was improved later by the addition of a clay rampart, strengthened with timber-laced walling which flanked its entrance. This was succeeded by a pair of ramparts and ditches.

The fort has a well-preserved souterrain built within the widened inner ditch space. The entrance at the N end leads into a 65-ft (19.8-m) long passage, the sides drystone walled. At the end is a roughly circular chamber nearly 12 ft (3.5 m) in diameter and 6 ft (1.8 m) high.

Castlerigg Bronze Age stone circle (NT guardianship of DE) *Cumbria, 1½ miles (2.4 km) E of Keswick* Pear-shaped in plan, this imposing circle, known as The Carles, has some 38 stones, most still standing, and within it is a rectangular setting of 10 stones which meet its circumference at the E. At the N a gap 11 ft (2.4 m) wide may have been an entrance.

Castlerigg stone circle, Cumbria

The Caterthuns (DE) *Menmuir, Tayside, 5 miles (8 km) NW of Brechin* These two Iron Age forts, standing within ¾ mile (1.2 km) of each other, are among the best known on Tayside. Both show signs of more than one structural period.

The **Brown Caterthun** appeared first as a small enclosure, 300 ft (94 m) by 200 ft (60.6 m), surrounded by a stone wall, the remains of which still exist. Outside this, enclosing 5 acres (2 ha), is a second ruined stone wall, then a double rampart and ditch. The nine entrances in these lines of defence plus an outer line of two more ramparts with eight entrances are a most puzzling feature.

The **White Caterthun** is enclosed by two massive concentric stone walls between 20 ft (6 m) and 40 ft (12.1 m) thick. These are inside a ditch and rampart with outer fortifications at a lower level.

The problems posed by these two peculiar strong points may not be solved until after they have been excavated.

CAVES AND ROCK SHELTERS

Aveline's Hole *Avon, near Burrington Combe* This cave is easily accessible from the road but caution is recommended to the explorer. There are two chambers, the inner one being approached through the outer. It furnished a comfortable shelter for men of the Upper Palaeolithic Age, between 25,000 and 10,000 BC. Flint implements, harpoons and possible human interments have been found here.

Cheddar Gorge *Somerset* Most of the caves in the Gorge have from time to time afforded shelter to hunters and food-gatherers in Palaeolithic times. The most accessible and most important one is **Gough's Cave (DE)** at the SW end. The outer portion of the cave has produced some thousands of tools, weapons and ornaments of flint, bone and shell, together with animal bones, all evidences of occupation between 25,000 and 10,000 BC.

Other caves, **Flint Jack's Cave, Soldier's Hole** etc., are not so easily accessible nor so profitable to visit.

Creswell Crags *Derbyshire, $\frac{1}{4}$ mile (0.4 km) E of Creswell* The B4062 road runs through the ravine called Creswell Crags. The caves in the rock faces were occupied periodically as shelters by palaeolithic and neolithic hunting peoples.

Church Hole on the S side of the Crags (in Nottinghamshire), a straight cave nearly 200 ft (60.6 m) long and 4 to 5 ft (1.2 to 1.5 m) wide, has yielded deposits dating from about 50,000 BC. to Roman times and after.

Mother Grundy's Parlour is U-shaped with a narrow passage leading off it. The remains of hearths and flint tools were found in it.

Pin Hole Cave is the smallest main cave, only 50 ft (15.2 m) long and quite narrow. It has produced valuable flints including the point of an ivory harpoon, a piece of bone with a human face engraved on it, and many flints.

Robin Hood's Cave had two main chambers and several smaller ones leading out of them. Tools and flint blades, and one piece of bone engraved with a horse's head were found in it.

Kent's Cavern (DE) *Devonshire, 1 mile (0.6 km) E of Torquay* This is one of the oldest inhabited caves in England, with two main chambers and many galleries, inhabited at times both by wild animals and by man. Implements and tools of all ages have been found in it.

Thor's Cave *Staffordshire $\frac{3}{4}$ mile (1.2 km) WSW of Wetton* Once inside the enormous entrance, the cave branches out in several directions. It was occupied, as remains found there show, well into the Roman period.

Victoria Cave *North Yorkshire, 1¾ miles (2.8 km) NE of Settle* This three-chambered cave was first inhabited by the hippopotamus, the woolly rhinoceros, elephant and hyena, then by bear, fox and red deer. Above the remains of these animals were found tools of the late Palaeolithic and Mesolithic ages.

The discovery of pottery, bronze brooches, jet and glass beads etc. denotes that the cave was apparently occupied during Roman times either as a place of refuge at times of invasion or as a robbers' hide-out.

Wookey Hole (DE) *Somerset, Wookey Hole village, 2 miles (3.2 km) N of Wells* The **Great Cave** was occupied during Roman times, the **Hyena Den** from the Ice Age to approximately 14,000 BC. In this cave the remains of hyenas and other wild animals have been found. Hunters who also used the cave left behind tools of flint and bone, and traces of fires lit in the cave.

Cawthorn Practice Camps *N. Yorkshire, 4 miles (6.4 km) N of Pickering* After the subjugation of the Brigantes in N Britain the 9th Hispana Legion was permanently stationed at York. During the reign of Trajan (AD 98–117) these legionaries probably constructed the four camps here.

They extend for ⅓ mile (0.5 km) along the edge of the Tabular Hills. From W–E (Camps D, C, A and B) the sites become less clearly marked. Camp D has double ditches and three entrances on W, S and E sides which are clearly marked. Its SE corner impinges on the western ditch of Camp C, a coffin-shaped enclosure covering 5 acres (2 ha). Farther east are Camps A and B.

Caynham Iron Age hill-fort *Salop, 2¼ miles (3.6 km) S of Ludlow* The well-preserved ramparts and the in-turned entrance at the E end of this rectangular fort make it well worth a visit. The enclosure of 8 acres (3.2 ha) is protected by a steep natural slope on the N, reinforced by a bank. The three other sides have bank, ditch and counterscarp bank, and on the W end where the ground is level these are strengthened by two extra banks, one inside the camp running N to S and the other outside, beyond the ramparts.

The Cerne Giant (NT) *Dorset, 1 mile (0.6 km) N of Cerne Abbas on Trundle Hill*   This is the most famous of all the ancient chalk-cut figures in England. Measuring 200 ft (60.9 m) from the sole of the foot to the end of the club he carries, he remains to remind us of our pagan ancestry. He has been described as an Iron Age fertility figure, as Corina, a companion of a Trojan prince who, expelled from Italy, settled in Albion (Britain) and as a representation of the Roman Emperor Commodus who assumed divinity and the title of Hercules Romanus. Whatever the explanation may be, many ancient legends and superstitions have grown up round this figure.

Chanctonbury Ring hill-fort *West Sussex, 6 miles (9.6 km) N of Worthing; 2½ miles (4 km) NW of Steyning*   Well-known because of its accessibility and as a fine viewpoint, this small enclosure is probably pre-Roman. Its 3½ acres (1.4 ha) are defended by bank and ditch and there is an entrance at the SW with an extra outer ditch on this side.

Two Roman buildings, one of these a smithy, another possibly a temple, with other structures, have been found within the fort.

Chesters Iron Age hill-fort *Lothian, ¾ miles (1.2 km) S of Drem*   This fort is unique in that it lies on lower land overlooked by a higher ridge. Its defences are impressive and its rampart well-preserved. Possibly it was not in danger of frequent assault and its formid-

Hand of Cerne Abbas Giant, Dorset

able defences were imposing enough to discourage attackers.

Cholesbury Camp hill-fort *Buckinghamshire, within Cholesbury village* The village church lies within the ramparts of this ancient 14-acre (5.5-ha) fort. Oval in plan, it has two banks and ditches on the N side and three on the S side. Excavation has disclosed two periods of construction in the 2nd and 1st centuries BC.

Cissbury Iron Age hill-fort (NT) *West Sussex, 3½ miles (5 km) N of Worthing* This 64-acre (26-ha) fort was re-fortified after the Roman evacuation of Britain in the 5th century AD, possibly to resist Saxon invaders. A number of neolithic flint-mines (c 2500–2000 BC) were enclosed within the western part of the fort. At about 250 BC the Iron Age people erected their ramparts round the site with an outer flat-bottomed ditch separated from it by a berm.

It was not used during Roman times, but the presence of 'Celtic' fields in and around it shows that farming went on there throughout the period.

93

Coldrum neolithic chambered long barrow (NT) *Kent, $3\frac{3}{4}$ miles (6 km) NE of Wrotham, 1 mile (1.6 km) NE of Trottiscliffe* and **Addington Park chambered long barrow** *$2\frac{1}{4}$ miles (3.6 km) E of Wrotham* These two barrows are sufficiently near each other to be considered together. The first is almost rectangular with a stone burial chamber at its E end in which at least 22 persons had been buried. Addington Park is also rectangular in plan, but the stones lying at its E end may represent either a false entrance or a burial chamber.

The remains of a third burial chamber, **The Chestnuts,** lie within $\frac{1}{4}$ mile (0.4 km) E of this but its original shape is not known.

Conderton Camp hill-fort *Hereford and Worcester, 6 miles (9.6 km) NE of Tewkesbury* This small but important fort, situated near the larger one at Bredon Hill, was constructed in about 150 BC as a cattle enclosure, defended by a simple bank and ditch with entrances at the S and N ends.

In the 1st century BC a stronger earthwork was made, cutting off about $2\frac{1}{2}$ acres (1 ha) enclosed by a bank of soil and rubble, with entrances S and N, and no ditch. The depressions inside this area are clear evidences of circular huts with storage pits, while inside the outer and earlier defences cattle were probably pastured. Stamped pottery taken from this camp and from Bredon Hill shows that they were probably inhabited by people of the same culture.

CORNWALL (WEST)
With the exception of Carn Brea, Halligye fogou, Harlyn Bay, The Hurlers, Rillaton barrow and Trethevy Quoit (see pages 87, 114, 115, 118, 134 and 174), all the most important sites, mainly prehistoric, are in the small peninsula no more than 5 miles (8 km) by 10 (16 km) west of a line from Penzance to St Ives.

This region has a character all its own and was open to influences from Ireland and the Continent. Almost all the burial chambers were enclosed by round barrows, probably neolithic. The varied nature of the terrain, heath inland, an easily accessible coast with hospitable valleys along the seaboard, together with a relatively mild climate, favoured settlement from neolithic times onwards. Hence here we have a 'little Britain' with all ages from neolithic to Roman represented in one way or another.

Ballowal (or Carn Gluze) neolithic chambered round barrow *1 mile (1.6 km) W of St Just* has a mound about 70 ft (20 m) across. Inside are concentric walls enclosing Bronze Age cists and pottery.

Boscawen-Un *1 mile (1.6 km) N of St Buryan* is one of the best Bronze Age stone circles in Cornwall, with 19 uprights and a centre stone.

Carn Euny Iron Age village and fogou *½ mile (0.8 km) NNW of Brane* In the last century BC a number of huts or small courtyard houses were built here. The most interesting feature of the settlement is the 66-ft (20-m) long fogou with a circular side chamber

Ballowal round barrow, Cornwall

Boscawen-Un stone circle, Cornwall

Carn Euny fogou, Cornwall

Lanyon Quoit, Cornwall

Chysauster Iron Age village, Cornwall

at the E end. This kind of construction corresponds in some respects to the souterrains of Scotland.

Chapel Euny neolithic chambered long barrow *Brane* The barrow, about 20 ft (6.1 m) in diameter and edged with upright stones, has an inner chamber entered at the SE and a roof of two capstones.

Chun Castle Iron Age hill-fort 2½ *miles (4 km) NE of St Just, 1 mile S of Morvah* This circular hill-fort is encircled by two granite-faced ramparts and two rock-cut ditches. The gaps through the banks to the SW entrance are staggered. Occupation lasted from the 2nd century BC into and after the Roman period.

Chun Quoit neolithic chambered tomb *just W of Chun Castle* The large burial chamber of four upright slabs is covered by an enormous 12-ft (2.4-m) square capstone. There are the remains of a barrow probably round, similar in character to Ballowal and Chapel Euny.

Chysauster Iron Age village (DE) 2 *miles (3.2 km) N of Trevarrack* A most interesting group of four pairs of courtyard houses lines a kind of village 'street'. Each courtyard is surrounded by a wall in the thickness of which a number of rooms open out on to the courtyard, resembling in some ways the ground plan of a Scottish broch. When excavated, some hearths were uncovered and many articles of household use were found.

Lanyon Quoit (NT) 2 *miles (3.2 km) SE of Morvah, on the N side of the Penzance Road* Here was once a neolithic long barrow. The capstone fell and in 1824 was replaced on top of the three uprights. Of the mound hardly a trace remains.

Men an Tol Bronze Age stone monument 1½ *miles (2.4 km) E of Morvah* The three stones are now in one straight line, but were once differently arranged. The middle stone has a large hole in it and has been thought to have been the entrance to a prehistoric burial chamber, but this cannot be proved.

Men an Tol, Cornwall

Merry Maidens Bronze Age stone circle *on S side of the B3315, immediately SW of Boleigh* Here are 19 4-ft (1.2-m) high standing stones (The Maidens) with a gap on the NE which may well have been the entrance. Nearly ¼ mile (0.4 km) NE, nearer to Boleigh are two large standing stones known locally as **The Pipers**. Legend has it that all were turned to stone for playing and dancing on a Sunday.

Mulfra Quoit *2 miles (3.2 km) S of Zennor* The mound of this neolithic barrow, possibly round, has disappeared, leaving a partially ruined burial chamber, its capstone leaning on the ground at its western end where there may once have been a fourth upright.

Treryn Dinas (Treen Dinas) Iron Age promontory fort (NT) *½ mile (0.8 km) S of Treen* The most northerly defence of this Iron Age fort, cutting off the headland, is a large bank and ditch. S of this are 3 smaller banks and ditches. The nearest fortification to the tip of the headland, and probably the latest, is another bank with a ditch outside it and a central causeway and entrance. Behind it is a circular hut site.

Mulfra Quoit, Cornwall

Zennor Quoit *1 mile (1.6 km) SE of Zennor* Two stones of this neolithic tomb, once probably covered by a circular mound, form a façade at the E end of the chamber. A single large slab divided the antechamber from the burial chamber, making it impossible to enter one from the other. The capstone over the burial chamber is supported by four large stones.

Crichton Iron Age souterrain *Lothian, 1 mile (1.6 km) E of Crichton village* Reached along a short passage about 50 ft (15.2 m) in length, 6 ft (1.8 m) broad and about 6 ft (1.8 m) high. Some parts of its ancient roof survive. On one of the lintels near the end of the passage is a carving of the front half of a winged horse. This and other stones are of Roman origin, probably brought here by the inhabitants from another site.

Croft Ambry Iron Age hill-fort (NT) *Hereford and Worcester, 2¼ miles (3.6 km) NE of Mortimer's Cross*

This triangular fort is protected by steep slopes on the N and W, two banks and ditches on the S and a counterscarp bank. Entrances on the E and W are approached by sunken tracks.

CROSBY IRON AGE VILLAGE SETTLEMENTS
Cumbria

On the hills bounded by the triangle Appleby–Shap–Kirkby Stephen are many village sites centring around **Crosby Garrett,** 3 miles (4.8 km) W of Kirkby Stephen and **Crosby Ravensworth**, 4 miles (6.4 km) E of Shap. All share the same characteristics.

The three villages of Crosby Garrett cover 160 acres (65 ha) and consist of hut enclosures and paddocks set among square fields. The main one, about 80 acres (37.3 ha), on the SE slope of Begin Hill has also a rectangular building with stone door-posts on its S side. The other two settlements are roughly 700 yd (640 m) and 1000 yd (914 m) NE of the first and only half its size.

Crosby Ravensworth has a series, probably pre-Roman in origin. Of these Burwens, 200 yd (183 m) NE of Crosby Lodge has hut foundations and a 'street' running SE from an entrance on the W side. Some of the huts back on the main enclosure wall and outside are 3–4 acres (1.2 to 1.6 ha) of 'fields'. Ewe Close, 1¼ acres (0.5 ha), has three enclosures with huts and paddocks, some with walls as high as 6 ft (1.8 m). Some Roman objects were found here. Ewe Locks, 1 acre (0.4 ha), has two groups of huts and paddocks and Howarcles, 1½ acres (0.6 ha), a series of oval and rectangular huts and paddocks alongside a 'street' running N–S. A further 2-acre (0.8-ha) settlement with some 20 hut foundations lies about 1000 yd (914 m) SE of it.

Danby Rigg, Bronze Age and Iron Age monuments
North Yorkshire South of Danby on the Esk, the

level of the land rises to a height of 1400 ft (410 m). On these slopes of Danby Rigg, a steep-sided spur contains some 800 very small circular mounds, probably once associated with burials, though none have so far been found there. A single standing stone 5 ft (1.5 m) high is the only remnant of a stone circle inside an earth bank. At its centre a cremation burial and two urns were found. The burial-ground is protected by a system of earthworks and near it is a group of banks enclosing what were probably 'Celtic' fields.

On the highest part of the moor, some 4¾ miles (7.6 km) S of Danby, is **Loose Howe**, an imposing round barrow 60 ft (18 m) in diameter which contained the remains of a man extended on a bed of reeds, rushes and straw, fully dressed in linen with leather shoes. An elegant canoe had been placed by his side. A second cremation burial was found E of the centre of the barrow and with it an urn, a stone battleaxe, a dagger blade and a pin.

Danebury Iron Age hill-fort *Hampshire, 3 miles (4.8 km) N of Stockbridge*   The earthworks lie under woodland, with some of the most complex defences in Britain. Essentially it is a two-banked fort built in the 4th century BC, and subsequently added to by improving banks and ditches, adding an enclosure on the SE, making a false or blocked entrance on the SW, while the true entrance with projecting earthworks on the NE is one of the most complicated ever constructed. It had a 'command post' from which any approach to the main gate could be reached by the defending slingers or archers. The whole work was finally encircled by an outermost rampart and ditch, and an outer gate added.

Danes' Graves *Nafferton, Humberside, 3½ miles (5 km) N of Driffield*   This, one of the most remarkable Iron Age barrow cemeteries in England, has been reduced by farming operations from about 500 to 200 mounds 10–30 ft (3–9 m) in diameter and 1–4 ft (0.3–1.2 m) high. Remains in crouched positions and grave goods have been found here, one burial being of two men with their chariot.

Deverel Bronze Age round barrow *Dorset, 1 mile (1.6 km) NE of Milborne* This bowl barrow is now encircled by a modern stone wall. It is famous, not for its appearance but for the goods found in it when it was excavated in 1824. These, together with those found at Rimbury (where nothing is to be seen today), gave the name 'Deverel-Rimbury' to a culture represented by a kind of barrel- and bucket-shaped urn.

Devil's Arrows *Boroughbridge, North Yorkshire* These huge Bronze Age standing stones, sited almost in a N–S line were brought from Knaresborough. They may originally have been part of the area of Bronze Age sacred sites which covered this region, extending S through Nunwick to the Thornborough, Hutton Moor and Cana sites.

THE DORSET CURSUS AND NEIGHBOURING SITES

On Thickthorn Down, 1 mile (1.6 km) NW of Gossage St Michael are two neolithic long barrows with U-shaped ditches. From a point near the larger of these two the Dorset Cursus runs in a NE direction for 6 miles (9.6 km). It is most clearly visible in the SW part of its course, especially where it encloses a neolithic long barrow to the point where it is cut by the Cranborne road.

Neolithic and Bronze Age peoples appear to have been attracted by this part of Dorset. Just W of the centre part of the Cursus, $\frac{3}{4}$ mile (1.2 km) E of Handley, stands **Wor Barrow long barrow**, which yielded six skeletons inside what had been a wooden structure.

103

The ditch has been completely cleared to its original depth—the only one in England to be thus exposed.

Immediately SE of the S end of the Cursus, 1 mile (1.6 km) NW of Gussage St Michael, are the two **Thickthorn long barrows,** the first with a horseshoe-shaped ditch which yielded neolithic pottery. On its SW side were later deposited remains of two women and a child accompanied by beakers and a copper awl. The second and larger barrow close to the S end of the Cursus also had a U-shaped ditch.

SE of the Cursus and $2\frac{3}{4}$ miles (4 km) SW of Cranborne, another group of henge monuments, the **Knowlton circles (DE)** in an almost straight line from NW to SE, are cut by the B3078 road. Part of the large S circle, 800 ft (244 m) in diameter, is occupied by a farm but the part behind the farm is still visible. The central circle 200 yd (183 m) to the N is smaller (106.7 m) and in its centre are the ruins of a Norman and later medieval church. The bank and inner ditch are clearly visible. The N circle is under the plough and now only visible from the air. In the field E of the central circle is a large round barrow now overgrown with trees, and the marks of many other barrows are visible from the air.

Returning to the Cursus we have, $1\frac{3}{4}$ miles (2.8 km) SE of Handley, one of the finest Bronze Age cemeteries in S England on **Oakley Down**. This consists of 25 barrows of the bowl, bell and disc types, which have yielded numerous articles of use and ornament. Two, both disc barrows, are cut by the **Ackling Dyke,** the Roman road from Old Sarum to Badbury Rings and Dorchester. Between Oakley Down and Wyke Down it is very well preserved, in places 40–50 (12.5–15.2 m) wide with a 10 ft (3 m) crown, rising 6–7 ft (1.8–2.1 m) above ground level and metalled with flint beach pebbles.

Finally, in the last days of Roman rule, **Bokerley Dyke,** one of the finest earthworks in Wessex, was constructed to protect the downland of N Dorset from invasion. This earthwork is cut by the A354 at its eastern end.

These sites, all within a short distance of each other, are not difficult to explore and are very rewarding.

Dreva Iron Age hill-fort *Borders, on Dreva Craig between Broughton and Stobo* The fort, in which the remains of hut foundations may be seen, stands on the summit, protected by stone walls. Outlying protection on the SW was given by a large number of pointed stones placed close together, probably intended to stop horsemen and chariots.

Duddo Bronze Age stone circle *Northumberland, ¾ mile (1.2 km) NNW of Duddo, on low-lying land close to the river Tweed* Only five stones, from 5 to 7 ft (1.5 to 2.1 m) are left of this small sacred site.

Duddo stone circle, Northumberland

Duggleby Howe neolithic round barrow *North Yorkshire, SE of Duggleby* One of the largest and certainly the most spectacular neolithic round barrows in Britain, still 20 ft (6.1 m) in height. Its great chalk mound once had an outer covering, also of chalk. In it was found a deep grave pit, above which there were 22 cremations and in the lower part some 10 more. In all, 53 were found, and there are probably others still undiscovered. Among the grave goods were bone pins, a flint knife, a mace head of antler, a flint axe and a bowl of neolithic pottery.

Edinburgh Though many Bronze Age burials and implements have been found within the boundaries of the city, open-air visible remains are few. In the S part are small standing stones, the most important being the Caiystane near Oxgangs Road, more than 9 ft (2.7 m) high with cup marks on one of its sides. Others are the Cat Stane at Kingsinch School and one in Ravenswood Avenue.

There are the remains of a cairn on Caerkerton Hill, and one at Gallachlaw. There were Iron Age fortifications on Salisbury Crags, Arthur's Seat and Dunsapie Hill in Holyrood Park.

The only Roman site within the city is the fort at Cramond (DE), part of which has been exposed. It was reconstructed by Severus because of the importance of its harbour for supplying the Antonine Wall.

Eggardon (Eggardun) Iron Age hill-fort *Dorset, 4¾ miles (7.6 km) ENE of Bridport* Approached by level land only on the NW and E, this is among the most spectacular forts in Wessex, with wide views on all sides. It was defended by three banks and ditches with more complicated earthworks at and outside its E entrance, and further defences in depth at the NW and down the hill slopes. Inside the enclosure are the remains of storage pits—an evidence of permanent occupation, several small mounds and two round barrows.

Eildon Hill fort and signal station *Borders, 1 mile (1.6 km) E of Melrose* Some 40 acres (16.2 ha) were enclosed by Iron Age people on the NE summit of the Eildon Hills, commanding the Tweed valley. It is believed to have been the capital of the Selgovae. Within its defences traces of 296 circular houses have been found, suggesting a population of some 2000. During the Roman period a signal station was built at the W end of this fort.

Eskdale Moor Bronze Age stone circles *Cumbria, on Burnmoor, 1 mile (1.6 km) NNW of Boot* The largest of the five circles, some 100 ft (30.4 m) in diameter, had 41 stones, most of them having fallen. The five cairns within this circle each contained a cremation. The other stone circles, much smaller, also had cairns with cremations.

A quarter of a mile (0.4 km) farther W are two more small circles, one containing one, the other two cairns.

Finavon vitrified hill-fort *Tayside, at the end of the Hill of Finavon* This oblong fort was first built during the 7th–6th centuries BC and is important to the archaeologist because of the vitrification by fire of part of its timber-laced wall. Inside the fort at the E and W ends were wells, and there are traces of hearths, indicating lean-to dwellings inside the N rampart.

Five Wells neolithic chambered tomb *Derbyshire, 1 mile (1.6 km) W of Taddington* This round barrow 1400 ft (427 m) above sea level commands a wide view of the surrounding landscape. It has two burial chambers set back to back, each approached by its own passage from the E and W ends. The roof slabs of both chambers are missing but the huge blocks of limestone around them still remain, the E chamber being the better preserved. The two pillars at the entry to this E chamber still stand; the W chamber is half buried and its portals have fallen against each other. At least 12 burials and some neolithic pottery and tools were found here.

Frensham Common Bronze Age bowl barrows (NT) *Surrey, 3¾ miles (6 km) NW of Hindhead* These are among the best preserved bowl barrows in Surrey. They vary in diameter from 42 ft (13 m) to 75 ft (23 m) and are from 4 ft (1.2 m) to 8 ft (2.4 m) in height. Some have surrounding ditches. Nothing is known of the contents.

Fyfield and Overton Downs Iron Age 'Celtic' fields *Wiltshire, on the path linking Avebury with Marlborough over the Downs* 'Celtic' fields are usually either invisible or barely visible on the ground, but this landscape provides one of the best examples on both sides of the path. In places boulders mark the lynchets, and banks where soil has washed down from higher levels are clearly visible.

Gatcombe Lodge neolithic chambered long barrow *Gloucestershire, 1 mile (0.6 km) N of Avening Church* This barrow, lying NE–SW has a false entrance at the NE end and a burial chamber on the N side near the E end. It is roofed by a capstone and there is some fine drystone walling inside. A large half-buried stone on the N side may have belonged to a second burial chamber.

A single standing stone called the **Long Stone** stands in an adjoining field and may have been part of another barrow.

Green Low neolithic chambered tomb *Derbyshire,*

1 mile (1.6 km) NW of Grangemill The round barrow resembled Five Wells (see page 107) in the same county, having a single burial chamber approached by a passage from the S. No burials are recorded, and this site was rifled in Roman times.

Hadrian's Wall near Chollerford

HADRIAN'S WALL (DE)

The Wall, which followed the line chosen by Hadrian as a frontier of the Roman Empire, lay between the Solway and the Tyne on ground most favourable to defence. Where there was a ridge the Wall followed its crest; where the ground was flat it was protected by a deep ditch and a berm between ditch and wall. All along the Wall at intervals of one Roman mile (about 1620 yd or 1.5 km) were small fortlets or milecastles each capable of housing 20 to 30 men, with gateways on N and S sides. Between each pair of mile-castles were two-storeyed turrets or lookout posts about 20 ft (6 m) square.

Before Hadrian's time the frontier had consisted of

a road (the **Stanegate**) running from the Tyne to the Solway with forts, fortlets and signal posts along its length. After the building of the Wall the forts were moved from the road up to the Wall itself. Finally an earthwork called the **vallum**, consisting of a wide flat-bottomed ditch with mounds both in front and behind it, was constructed on the Roman side of the Wall as a rear line of defence and a means of controlling traffic through its many gates.

At the end of Hadrian's reign (AD 138) the Wall had been extended on the E to Wallsend, much of the turf wall on its western end had been rebuilt in stone and there were 16 forts along its length. The vallum behind it had been completed, there were outpost forts occupied by Roman forces protecting its northern approaches and a system of roads, forts, posting and supply stations to the S.

For a time after AD 143 the Wall was supplanted by the Antonine Wall farther N, but 20 years later the Scottish Lowlands were evacuated except for some outposts; the final 26 miles (42 km) of the turf wall were replaced by stone, the fort of **Chesterholm** on the Stanegate was reconstructed and the **Military Way** was made, running between the Wall and the vallum, connecting all the forts, with branches to the milecastles and to the Stanegate behind the defence system.

Military disasters followed. For a time the Antonine Wall was reoccupied. In AD 208 Hadrian's Wall was rebuilt by Severus and though overrun and partially abandoned at times, remained the official frontier of the Roman Empire until the Roman withdrawal from Britain.

For the complete or even partial exploration of the Wall, the Ordnance Survey Map or the Map of the Wall published by H.M.S.O. is necessary.

From E–W the Wall only becomes visible at **Denton** where stands **Turret 7b**, well preserved and 4 ft

(1.2 m) high. The most worthwhile section near the E end is at **Heddon-on-the-Wall** where it is 9 to 10 ft (2.7 to 3.0 m) wide and 7 ft (2.1 m) high. The best preserved sections are near **Housesteads** and **Greatchesters forts.** Along and W of this stretch are several turrets and milecastles still existing. Some of the principal places to visit are listed below.

Benwell (Condercum) just north of the town, has the only crossing of the vallum visible today. Near it are the remains of a small temple dedicated to the god Antenociticus.

Birdoswald (Camboglanna) (DE) *1¼ miles (2 km) W of Gilsland on the western stretch of the frontier* None of the buildings inside this 5¼-acre (2.1-ha) fort can now be seen but the ramparts are still there. Particularly impressive is the E gate. From the NW corner of the fort the Wall extends westwards to **Turret 49b.** Here the earlier turf wall ran S of the stone wall and can be made out in places.

East of the fort the Wall runs down to the Irthing. Because the river has changed course, part of the Roman bridge (DE) that ran over it is still visible at low water. Further E between Willowford and Gilsland there are more views of Wall, ditch and **Turrets (48b, 48a)** and **milecastle 48** (at Gilsland), a particularly well-preserved example.

Carrawborough (Procolitia) (DE) *on the B6318 4 miles (6.4 km) W of Chollerford* Not much remains, but SW of the fort are the remains of the temple dedicated to Mithras, one of the few to be excavated. 100 yd (91.4 m) W of the fort are the remains of a shrine to the water goddess Coventina with the 7-ft (2.1-m) deep well from which a large number of coins, votive offerings etc. were recovered.

Chesterholm (Vindolanda) (DE) *S of the B6318, 5 miles (8 km) NNW of Haltwhistle* The visible remains of this 3½-acre (1.4-ha) fort founded by

Agricola, abandoned under Hadrian and rebuilt by Severus and Constantius, consist of the headquarters building, walls on the W and E, and the two gates N and W. Directly W of the fort are the remains of the civilian settlement which was reached by means of a road running from the W gate.

To show the visitor what the Roman fort really looked like, reconstructions of three demonstration sections are now (1975) being carried out and these include a 15-yd (13.7-m) stone wall with a 6-ft (1.8-m) parapet and turret, a 15-ft (4.6-m) high wall with a timber parapet and a timber milecastle gateway. There are also replicas of Roman war machines.

Important information is being gained on life in and around the forts of the Roman Wall.

Chesters (Cilurnum) (DE) *S of the B6316,* $\frac{1}{2}$ *mile (0.8 km) SW of Chollerford above the N. Tyne* The fort, covering almost 6 acres (2.4 ha), was built before the completion of the Wall and designed for cavalry,

Chesters Roman fort, Hadrian's Wall

but was used for infantry until the 3rd century. All the gates and some of the towers are open for inspection, as are also the headquarters, commanding officer's house and some barrack blocks. East of the fort near the river bank are the remains of the bath-house with the foundations of all the rooms. It is one of the best-preserved buildings of its kind in Britain.

Near Chesters are other visible remains including the eastern abutment of the bridge across the North Tyne. A little farther east across the B6079 is **Turret 26b**, one of the best preserved, with a 60-yd (54.8-m) stretch of the Wall, 8 ft (2.4 m) high in places.

Corbridge (Corstopitum) (DE) Here there was not only a fort built by Agricola, but also a flourishing town, base and arsenal from which a large section of the Wall was supplied. Most of the visible remains go back to the rebuilding of the fort by Severus. The Stanegate (E–W) ran through the town. On view are two granaries with raised floors and beside them an aqueduct with its fountainhead, a 1-acre (0.4-ha) site believed to have been an unfinished storehouse, and on the S side of the Stanegate, headquarters buildings, officers' houses, stores, an ordnance depot with workshops, and temples. Models and exhibits are in the museum on the site.

Greatchesters (Aesica) *2 miles (3.2 km) N of Halt-whistle via a minor road N of the B6318* This 3-acre (1.2-ha) fort, built about AD 128, replaced a milecastle. Only the outlines of its ditch, ramparts and gates are visible. In the 4th century the W gate was blocked for some reason and its blocking walls are still in position. Inside are the remains of 4th-century barrack rooms, but not much is known about other internal buildings.

Three-quarters of a mile (1.2 km) E of Greatchesters over the Haltwhistle Burn is **Milecastle 62** with 6-ft (2.4-m) thick walls still standing six courses high. From Greatchesters the line of the Wall runs westwards to **Milecastle 44**, 1 mile (1.6 km) and **Turret 44b**,

Housesteads Roman fort, Hadrian's Wall

$1\frac{3}{4}$ miles (2.8 km), with the well-preserved vallum seen to the S.

Housesteads (Vercovicium) (NT under guardian-ship of DE) *off the B6318, 5 miles (8 km) E of Great-chesters, 2 miles (3.2 km) NE of Chesterholm* House-steads replaced Chesterholm when Hadrian built the Wall. The 5-acre (2-ha) fort has been well excavated and the headquarters, hospital, commanding officer's house, granaries, one barrack block and a latrine at the SE corner are visible.

To the W of the fort the Wall may be clearly seen. Here **Milecastle 37** is one of the best preserved, and beyond it more of the Wall and mounds marking the site of **Milecastle 38**. There are further stretches of the Wall and the remains of milecastles between here and Greatchesters. (See Back Endpaper.)

Halligye fogou *Cornwall, 4 miles (6.4 km) SE of Helston* The Iron Age fortified homestead and its ditch having entirely disappeared, only the fogou, considered to be the finest in Cornwall, remains. It is roughly T-shaped, with the stem of the T lying E–W, 54 ft (16.5 m) long and roofed with stone slabs. The cross of the T, running N–S used to open into a low chamber and then on to the homestead ditch at its N end. This outlet is now blocked. The modern entrance is at the W end of the main passage. It has a small passage running S here and a ridge across the main passage, possibly to deceive or trip up intruders.

Ham Hill Iron Age hill-fort *Somerset, 4¾ miles (7.6 km) W of Yeovil* This large 210-acre (85-ha) fort occupies the whole of the hill. It is enclosed for the most part by two banks and ditches, and by triple banks and ditches on the NE and SW. Extensive and probably permanent occupation has yielded goods in large quantities, but the site has been damaged by quarrying from Roman times onwards.

Hambledon Hill causewayed camp, barrows and hill-fort *Dorset, ¾ mile (1.2 km) N of Child Okeford* In neolithic times there was a causewayed camp here, enclosed by a double bank and ditch. NW of this the Iron Age people erected one of the finest hill-forts in Wessex, with triple ramparts except on the S, enclosing about 25 acres (10 ha). There are entrances on the N, NE and SW, the last two being staggered. Within the hill-fort there is a long barrow.

Harlyn Bay Cemetery *Cornwall, 2½ miles (4 km) W of Padstow* This Iron Age cemetery had more than 100 cists made of local slate, each grave containing a skeleton in a crouched position. A museum on the site contains the articles discovered, and five of the graves are preserved in the ground. It is open in summer during limited hours.

Hembury Causewayed Camp and hill-fort *Devon, 3½ miles (5.6 km) NW of Honiton* Here a 7-acre

Ham Hill, Somerset

Hambledon Hill, Dorset

(2.8-ha) Iron Age hill-fort was built over a much earlier neolithic causewayed camp. The hill-fort had three banks and ditches on W and N, two on the E, with entrances on the W side and at the NE corner. The neolithic camp occupied the S half of the fort but its existence was not suspected until the excavations of 1930–5, and nothing can now be seen of it.

Hengistbury Head Iron Age promontory fort *Dorset, on the coast S of Christchurch* This fort was defended by earthworks dug across the peninsula, with double banks extending some 1500 ft (457 m). It protected Christchurch harbour. There is a central entrance gap 18 ft (5.5 m) wide. Here are a number of bowl barrows, seven on the Head, two on lower ground, one of the latter producing valuable finds.

Hetty Pegler's Tump, neolithic chambered long barrow (DE) *Gloucestershire, 1 mile (0.6 km) N of Uley Church* The peculiar name of this barrow is that of a 17th-century owner of the high ridge on which it stands. It is approached by a deep forecourt, has an underground passage 22 ft (6.7 m) long, with two chambers on each side of which only those on the S side are visible. At the end is a fifth chamber. Altogether 24 skeletons were found here.

Hob Hurst's House, Bronze Age barrow (DE) *Derbyshire, 3 miles (4.8 km) SE of Baslow* The barrow is more rectangular than round and has a mound some 4 ft (1.2 m) high. When excavated in 1853 a stone cist 10 ft by 9 ft (3 by 2.7 m) was found in the centre, with burnt bones in one corner of it.

Hod Hill Iron Age hill-fort and Roman fort *Dorset, 3¾ miles (6.0 km) NW of Blandford* In the NE corner of the evacuated hill-fort the Romans constructed a permanent fort. This is the only example of its kind in Britain. Its 50 acres (20.2 ha) were defended by multiple ditches, still clearly marked, with entrances at the NE and SW. In early Roman times part of a legion and some cavalry were stationed here, and foundations of some of the buildings have been discovered.

Holkham Iron Age lowland fort *Norfolk, 3 miles (4.8 km) ESE of Wells-next-the-Sea*   This and another fort at Warham are included because of their peculiar character. Holkham, roughly oval, is built on an island in a tidal salt marsh, with a bank and ditch on the NE and two banks with a ditch between them on the S. Enclosing $5\frac{1}{2}$ acres (2.2 ha), it is believed to have acted as a protection for a coastal trading station.

The Hurlers Bronze Age stone circles *Cornwall, $1\frac{1}{2}$ miles (2.4 km) W of Upton Cross*   These three spectacular stone circles stand in a line NE–SW each being over 100 ft (30.4 m) in diameter. Excavation has proved that they were dressed to shape and sunk half their length in ground packed with granite blocks.

Ilkley Moor Bronze Age stone carvings, circles and cairns *W Yorkshire, S of Ilkley, on the moors*   Scattered about the moor, mainly near its northern edge, are numerous stones decorated with incised markings, and on the E side are a number of burial sites and monuments. On **Baildon Hill,** S of Ilkley Moor and $\frac{1}{2}$ mile (0.8 km) NE of Baildon is another group of cup and ring marked rocks.

Ingleborough Iron Age hill-fort *N Yorkshire, NE of Ingleton*   The fort stands on the very summit of Ingleborough at a height of 2350 ft (716 m), a worthwhile excursion for good climbers. The site is protected by natural rocks reinforced by boulders brought to the spot, put in place and backed by others. The

The Hurlers, Cornwall

outer rampart is now defaced, stones having been taken in modern times to build a cairn. The NW and S entrances and some hut foundations are still visible.

Kestor Bronze Age village settlement *Devon, 2½ miles (4 km) SW of Chagford* This, an easily accessible site (the Chagford–Batworthy road passes through it), is on the slope of the hill crowned by Kestor rock. The 25 circular huts had stone-wall footings and roofs supported on central posts. To the W of the road is Round Pound, a circular enclosure with an entrance on the NW. In it was a hut 37 ft (11.2 m) in diameter which had a ring of posts supporting the roof, a hearth, a furnace and a forging pit.

King Arthur's Round Table and Mayborough neolithic sacred sites (DE) *Cumbria, 1¼ miles (2 km) SE of Penrith on the S side of Eamont Bridge* The Round Table, in the SW angle of the A6 and A592 junction, is a circular enclosure with a surrounding ditch. It had two original entrances but only the one on the SE now remains.

Mayborough (DE), ¼ mile (0.4 km) to the W, with a rampart formed of stones, encloses about 1½ acres

Kits Coty, Kent

(0.7 ha). Near the centre is a high stone. There were four stones here in the mid 19th century and four more flanking the entrance.

Kits Coty neolithic chambered long barrow *Kent, 5¼ miles (8.4 km) S of Rochester* This mound and Lower Kits Coty ¼ mile (0.4 km) S of it, have been so denuded that their dimensions cannot be given. Three uprights and a capstone remain of the former, and of the latter only a heap of about 20 stones.

Knap Hill neolithic causeway camp and Iron Age enclosure *Wiltshire, 3½ miles (5.6 km) NW of Pewsey* This neolithic earthwork encloses about 4 acres (1.6 ha) and has many causeways breaking the bank and ditch. The earthwork is well defined on the NE and where the slope is less steep.

On the E side a rectangular earthwork encloses ½ acre (0.2 ha) of land, and once protected an Iron Age farmstead.

Lacra Bronze Age stone circles *Cumbria, 1½ miles (2.4 km) NW of Millom, ½ mile (0.8 km) E of Kirksanton* Once a Bronze Age religious centre, Lacra contains five stone circles. One circle had a central mound on which was an inner ring of stones, and a large flat stone lies near the centre of another. The lines of two possible avenues have been made out but these are confused owing to the number of natural rocks which lie near them.

On the S side of Kirksanton are two standing stones known as the **Giant's Grave**. The larger stone has incised cup-marks on it.

Lambourn Bronze Age barrow cemetery *Berkshire, 2½ miles (4 km) N of Lambourn* The barrows lie on and near the Lambourn–Kingston Lisle road. Altogether there are more than 40, but only those beside the road are accessible. These are of various kinds and contained a variety of grave goods when excavated.

Just N of the group is a neolithic long barrow standing at the S end of a wood. It was found to contain a burial and some perforated sea shells.

Lambourn barrow cemetery, Berkshire

Leckhampton Hill Iron Age promontory fort
Gloucestershire, $2\frac{1}{2}$ miles (4 km) S of Cheltenham
Steep slopes, now made steeper by quarrying, protected this fort on the N and W. On the S and E was a bank and a rock-cut ditch with an outer bank and ditch, now overgrown. The entrance, a passage-way 10 ft (3 m) wide, is on the E side.

Outside the fort near the entrance is a round barrow which may be contemporary with the fort.

London (Londinium)   The situation of London near the mouth of the Thames, easily accessible from the Continent made it the principal town and the largest in area in all Roman Britain. Its importance as a centre of trade and administration may be seen from a glance at a map of the Roman roads that radiated from it, much as do the roads of today.

Pressure on land plus centuries of building and rebuilding on the site has obliterated or covered up most of what Rome left behind, and the chief remains still accessible and in place are those of the Wall, the Cripplegate fort, a house and a tessellated pavement.

Excavation has revealed the probable line of some of the streets, the plans of several buildings, the site of the basilica and forum between Cornhill and Fenchurch Street, and an imposing building on and near the site of the present Cannon Street Station which may have been the residence or headquarters of an important official or governor.

The earliest Roman fortification in stone was a fort of the usual pattern covering some 12 acres (4.8 ha) at Cripplegate, with its main streets NE and SW and defended by a wall, ditch and rampart. Foundations of the fort are still visible in Noble Street and the West Gate (entrance now in London Wall).

Some time between AD 190 and 210 a wall was built round the entire town, and this, existing up to Stuart times, determined its future shape. The English names

122

Roman city wall, London Wall

of the gates still survive. It may be seen S of the church-yard of St Giles, Cripplegate, in the PO yard, St Martins le Grand, in St Alphege churchyard (off London Wall), in Coopers Row (between Tower Hill and Crutched Friars, EC3), in Trinity Place (EC3) and in the Tower. In places medieval building is above the Roman lower courses.

There are the remains of a Roman house with baths in Lower Thames Street and a tessellated floor in All Hallows, Barking Church.

In 1954 the remains of a Mithraic temple were found during excavations in Walbrook (EC4). Owing to building operations, these had to be removed and reconstructed on the SE side of Queen Victoria Street where they are now on view.

What is lacking in sites on view to the public is to a great extent made up for by the wealth of material excavated and placed in London museums. These, together with maps, plans and models may be seen in the British Museum, the Museum of London in London Wall and others.

Long Meg and daughters, Cumbria

Long Meg and her Daughters *Cumbria, ¾ mile (1.2 km) NE of Little Salkeld* This is one of the best stone circles in the north, with originally about 70 stones, now 51 (the Daughters) of which 27 are standing. Long Meg, 12 ft (3.6 m) high, stands a short way NW of her 'family' and has cup and ring incised marks on one face. There are traces of a bank on the W side and there are two more outlying stones between Long Meg and the circle.

Lydney hill-fort, iron mines and Roman temple *Gloucestershire, in Lydney Park, 1 mile (1.6 km) S of Lydney* An Iron Age earthwork defends a spur which looks S towards the Severn. In the 2nd and 3rd centuries AD iron was mined here, and the shaft of one of the workings is still visible, jutting through the rampart.

In the 4th century a rectangular temple was erected to Nodens, god of healing, near the S point of the spur. A bath suite and guesthouse catered for patients.

The site is on private land and exhibits are in Lydney Park private museum.

Maiden Castle *Dorset, $1\frac{3}{4}$ miles (2.8 km) SW of Dorchester* One of the best-known and most remarkable sites in the whole of the British Isles, the eastern part of the hill on which Maiden Castle stands was first enclosed by neolithic peoples as a causewayed camp. Overlying this were found the remains of a very long barrow, 1800 ft (548 m), at the eastern end of which were discovered the remains of a man whose body had been hacked to pieces after death.

After about 1800 BC the site became uninhabited. The first Iron Age ramparts were erected round about 300 BC and enclosed 15 acres (6 ha) on the E side of the hill. More than a century later the ramparts were extended to cover the whole 45 acres (18.2 ha), and within the fort a large population had its permanent home.

Maiden Castle, Dorset

Early in the 1st century BC new immigrants rebuilt the ramparts, adding an outer bank and ditch, remodelling the entrances and creating the complicated ways between the strong points round the gates. Between 43 and 47 AD during the Roman advance to the W, the fort was stormed by the Romans, the E gate destroyed and later the population was re-housed in the Roman town of Durnovaria (Dorchester). In the 4th century, at the E end, a Celtic-type temple was erected and a small house adjoined it. From the air the fortifications may be seen in all their complexity.

Merrivale Bronze Age stone monuments *Devon, 4 miles (6.4 km) E of Tavistock, on the S side of the A384* Two double parallel stone rows run from W to E, the northern one 596 ft (181 m) long, blocked by a stone at the E end, the southern one 865 ft (264 m) long with a small cairn ringed by a stone circle breaking the line. There is a large stone cist to the SE, a stone circle to the SW and groups of hut circles on both sides of the road.

Merrivale stone monuments, Devon

Midsummer and Hollybush Hills Iron Age hill-fort (NT) *Hereford and Worcester, 2 miles (3.2 km) SSW of Little Malvern* This irregularly shaped 30-acre (12-ha) fort has in-turned entrances at the N and SW. The hollows inside the fort probably represent hut foundations. At the N end of Hollybush Hill is a neolithic long barrow with ditches still visible and a short distance N of it are three round barrows.

MINES, QUARRIES AND INDUSTRIAL SITES

Hundreds of these have been found all over the island, but few have enough to show to make them worth a visit. With very few exceptions industry in prehistoric Britain was on a small scale and traces have been lost. Many Roman establishments have also been obliterated by later developments, but the wares they produced are to be seen in museums. A few sites which are worth visiting are given here, and intending visitors should be prepared to walk some way, and in the case of mines, to be suitably clothed and to carry torches.

Charterhouse-on-Mendip mining settlement *Avon* Lead was being mined here before the arrival of the Romans, and they were quick to exploit this and other local sites. By AD 49 pigs bearing the name of the Roman Emperor were being produced. A Roman road ran from here to Old Sarum, and may have extended westwards to the Bristol Channel at Uphill. All that can be seen today are the remains of a small amphitheatre, some rectangular enclosures and traces of the Old Sarum road.

Dolaucothi gold mines *near Pumpsaint, Dyfed, ¾ mile (1.2 km) SE of the village* The Romans were quick to realize the value of the gold deposits in and around the valleys of the Cothi and Annell rivers, and a speedy development of the workings followed within a few years of the conquest. This consisted of both opencast and underground workings plus a system of aqueducts brought from the River Cothi for washing the ore. Reservoirs and the courses of aqueducts may be seen, and many of the casts are still open.

Grimes Graves flint mines (DE) *Norfolk, 5½ miles (8.8 km) NW of Thetford*   This extensive system of more than 350 neolithic mines provided material for weapons and tools which were exported in a rough state all over the country. The flint was dug from bell-shaped pits where it was near the surface, and from deeper workings with galleries radiating from them. Implements for digging were the bones and antlers of deer, and flint wedges to prize out the lumps. The general method was, when the workings of one pit were exhausted, to fill it with the material dug when opening the next. One of the pits was found to contain a votive shrine.

Lydney iron mines see Lydney hill-fort, page 124

Pike of Stickle axe factory *Cumbria, 3¼ miles (5.2 km) NNW of Chapel Stile on N side of Great Langdale*   Here on the slope leading up to the Pike are to be found flint flakes, axe-heads shaped in the rough, and debris lying about. The material, hard in texture and easy to flake, appears to have been used only for axe-heads which reached all parts of Britain, especially the SW.

Sussex flint mines   Though not on the scale of Grimes Graves (see above), there were several places in W Sussex where flint was mined and shaped. About 100 shafts were dug at **Blackpatch Hill**, 1¾ miles (2.8 km) W of Findon, though only a few low hollows are to be seen today. There were also pits at **Cissbury** near the Iron Age hill-fort on W and S. The largest group on **Harrow Hill**, 2¾ miles NW of Findon, had both deep and opencast diggings.

Mitchell's Fold Bronze Age stone circle (DE) *Salop, 5 miles (8 km) NW of Lydham, nr Chirbury* Some of the original 16 stones are visible here, now reduced to ground level. From this site there are extensive views, especially to the W towards Wales.

The Mutiny Stones *Borders, 4¼ miles (6.8 km) NNW of Longformacus* In the moorland of the Lammermuir Hills, this neolithic cairn is one of the most impressive in northern Britain. A stretch of drystone walling was found inside it, but there was no trace of a burial chamber. Though despoiled, the cairn still stands to a height of 8 ft (2.4 m) at its E end.

Nine Barrows *Dorset, 2¼ miles (3.6 km) ESE of Corfe Castle* A neolithic long barrow here became the focal point of a group of Bronze Age bowl barrows. It now stands near the E end and the round barrows are in a line on a S-facing ridge. The largest, still 100 ft (30.5 m) across and 10 ft (3 m) high, has a clearly visible ditch 10 ft (3 m) wide all round it.

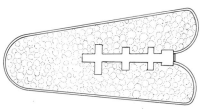

Plan of chambered long barrow

Nine Stones Bronze Age stone circle (DE) *Dorset, ½ mile (0.8 km) W of Winterbourne Abbas* Standing on the S side of the A35, this small stone circle is easily accessible, and has stones of varying height from 1 to 7 ft (0.3 to 2.1 m) of various irregular shapes.

Nine Stones, Dorset

Normans Law Iron Age hill-fort *Fife, 5½ miles (8.9 km) NW of Cupar* This fort is believed to have been the capital of the Celtic tribe of the Venicones. It is a stone 'ring fort' at the highest point of a hill and had a wall between 10 ft and 16 ft (3 m and 4.9 m) thick. There are traces of earlier defences outside the fort, including a wide ditch that runs round the SW foot of the hill.

Notgrove neolithic long barrow (DE) *Gloucestershire, 4¼ miles (6.8 km) NW of Bourton-on-the-Water* This important but badly defaced barrow had a forecourt between 'horns' of drystone walling, a gallery and two pairs of side-chambers leading from it. At its end was a circular chamber. All these chambers are now unroofed. Finds included nine adults and one child, neolithic pottery and ornaments. In the forecourt were found the remains of fires.

Nympsfield neolithic chambered long barrow *Gloucestershire, 4¼ miles (6.8 km) SW of Stroud* The Nympsfield barrow conforms to the Cotswold type, with a forecourt at the E end between two 'horns', an antechamber, two side chambers and an end chamber. The drystone wall round the barrow is hidden under the mound and the roof is missing. There were evidences of fires in the forecourt and at the W end there were post-holes indicating the presence of some kind of building. The remains of 20 persons have been found here together with neolithic pottery and an arrowhead.

Oldbury Camp Iron Age hill-fort *Warwickshire, 3½ miles (5.6 km) W of Nuneaton* The smallest in area of six hill-forts in this county, Oldbury is among the best preserved. Its bank and ditch enclosed some 7 acres (2.8 ha) and can still be seen on most of the circumference, the bank in places being 6 ft (1.8 m) high. The original entrance has not been found.

Oldbury Hill Iron Age hill-fort (NT) *Kent, ¾ mile (1.2 km) SW of Ightham* The natural slopes protecting this large 123-acre (49-ha) fort were reinforced by a rampart still visible on all sides except on the NE where levelling has taken place, and at the steep E end. In places there was an outer ditch. Entrances were on the S and NE. The camp was probably constructed at about 100 BC and some 50 years later the ditch was deepened, additional ramparts were added and an in-turned entrance was made. On the E side of the fort 400 yd (365 m) S of its NE entrance there are the remains of Old Stone Age rock shelters, probably dating back beyond 100,000 BC, and many implements have been found there.

Old Oswestry Iron Age hill-fort (DE) *Salop, 1 mile (1.6 km) N of Oswestry* This fort compares with any in Britain for the complexity of its defences and its state of preservation. The hill appears to have been occupied in the 3rd century BC, though the fort was not built until about 100 years later, and probably developed in four stages, first a double bank and ditch with entrances E and W, then a third bank on all sides except the SE; then a reconstruction of the W entrance, the digging of a number of pits and the making of a sunken entrance 100 yd (91.4 m) long at that side. Finally the site was encircled by two more banks and ditches with a flanking bank constructed to protect an E entrance. This last was added about the time of the Roman conquest.

Oxton Camp Iron Age hill-fort *Nottinghamshire, 1¼ miles (2 km) NE of Oxton* This hill-fort and the Bronze Age barrow outside the NE entrance are the only prehistoric sites of any importance in the county. The fort is small, enclosing only 1½ acres (0.6 ha) with a bank, ditch and counterscarp bank on the W, and three banks and ditches on the E. There was an entrance on the NW side and probably another at the SE. The barrow is large, about 90 ft (27.4 m) in diameter and 20 ft (6 m) high. Locally it was named Robin Hood's Pot, and Roman coins were dug up there.

Parc-le-Breos (Parc Cwm) neolithic chambered long barrow *W Glamorgan, 1 mile (1.6 km) N of Parkmill (Gower Peninsula)* This is an early example of the type of burial chamber found in S Wales. It is short in comparison with its width, has a deep forecourt from which a gallery leads to two pairs of side chambers and there is no false entrance.

Pentre Ifan neolithic chambered long barrow (DE) *Dyfed, 1¼ miles (2 km) N of Brynberian* The most imposing feature of this monument is the massive capstone resting on three uprights. The mound, originally 130 ft (39.6 m), is no longer there, but there is a semicircular forecourt lined with stone slabs, a portal of two tall stones with a shorter one between them. There were no side chambers.

Old Oswestry hill-fort, Salop

Pentre Ifan long barrow, Dyfed

Pimperne neolithic long barrow *Dorset, 3 miles (4.8 km) NE of Blandford*   The traveller on the A354 cannot miss this 330-ft (100.5-m) long mound, one of the longest in Dorset. It is 11 ft (2.4 m) high and the side-ditches, separated from it by broad berms and not meeting at the end, are visible all along its length.

Priddy Bronze Age circles and barrows, and Ashen Hill barrows *Somerset, 4½ miles (7.2 km) N of Wells*   The four sacred sites at Priddy are unique in that the bank is inside the ditch, a feature only seen elsewhere at Stonehenge. They are all about 600 ft (183 m) in diameter and extend in a line N to S.

Three-quarters of a mile (1.2 km) S of the circles and probably associated with them are seven barrows with two more separated from them on the N. The line of barrows curves S from N to E, and all are large and conspicuous. They all probably contained cremation burials at one time.

Just N of these barrows are more of the same kind, stretching in a row nearly E to W. All are large and, excavated at various times, have yielded cremation burials, urns, beads, daggers and a cup.

Rainsborough Camp Iron Age hill-fort *Northamptonshire, 5¾ miles (9.3 km) SE of Banbury (Oxfordshire)*   This is the best preserved of three hill-forts in this county. Roughly oval in plan, it encloses some 6 acres (2.4 ha), defended by a bank, ditch and counterscarp bank. An outer ditch has been filled in. Excavation has revealed the only certain entrance on the W side, which was complex, with a 60-ft (18.3-m) long passage.

Rillaton Bronze Age round barrow *Cornwall, just N of The Hurlers, near St Cleer*   This barrow is notable for the inhumation burial found in it, accompanied by a ribbed gold cup with a handle very much like those found at Mycenae in S Greece, a dagger, pottery and glass beads. It is 8 ft (2.4 m) high, with a cavity in the top, and E of the centre there still remains the stone burial cist which contained the remains.

Rollright Stones (DE) *Oxfordshire, ½ mile (0.8 km) NE of Little Rollright, 2½ miles (4 km) N of Chipping Norton* This group is the most famous in the county and the names indicate the legends that have grown up around them. **The King's Men** is a circle of about 70 stones, and just east of it stands the **King Stone** on the Warwickshire side of the road. It is 8 ft (2.4 m) high and 5 ft (1.5 m) wide and is probably an isolated Bronze Age standing stone.

East of the Rollright stones are the probable remains of a long barrow now known as the **Whispering Knights.** Here four upright stones form a chamber about 6 ft (1.8 m) square and a fifth stone, probably a capstone, leans beside them at an angle.

Rillaton round barrow, Cornwall

Rollright Stones, Oxfordshire

ROMAN BARROWS

The Bartlow Hills *Essex, on the road between Ashdon* (*Essex*) *and Bartlow* (*Cambridgeshire*) Four of the original eight hills were removed in 1832 to clear the ground for agriculture. The eastern line, 21 to 40 ft high (7.6 to 12.2 m) running N to S, still exists. It was believed at one time without justification that they were associated with the great battle of Ashingdon (or Assandune) between Edmund Ironside and Canute.

From the levelled barrows were taken drinking vessels, burnt human bones and coins; from those that still remain, a bronze bowl, an iron lamp, a folding stool, perfume bottles, Samian pottery, human bones and many other articles. Many relics were lost when Easton Lodge was destroyed by fire in 1847. The barrows were obviously tombs belonging to wealthy and powerful families, probably romanized British.

Mersea Island barrow *Essex, at Barrow Hill Farm, on L fork of the B1025 which enters the island* Smaller

136

than the largest of the Bartlow Hills, this 20-ft (6.1-m) high barrow when excavated revealed a square brick vault in which was a leaden casket containing a globular urn of green glass containing human bones.

ROMAN FORTS AND SIGNAL STATIONS

Roman forts were built in various parts of the country but especially where there was the possibility of attack either from enemies outside or rebellious tribesmen—hence they are more frequently found nearer the Scottish border and in Wales.

Many have long since disappeared and, as in the case of Great Casterton (Leicestershire) and Water Newton (Cambridgeshire) have only been found by aerial photography. In two notable examples, Hod Hill (Dorset) and Woden Law (Borders), Roman works have been put on sites of Iron Age hill-forts.

Roman forts were designed to hold up to 500 men. They needed strong defences and reasonably comfortable quarters, therefore they were solidly built, designed for permanent occupation. They follow the standard design—rectangular, with round corners, plus the usual plan of streets and buildings.

Brecon Gaer (DE) *Powys, 3 miles (4.8 km) W of Brecon*   A most important 8-acre (3.2-ha) fort in the heart of S Wales which was occupied from the 1st to the 4th centuries AD. Its walls and buildings were constructed in stone in the 2nd century. It had two ditches and its ramparts are still visible. In front of the headquarters building along the main street was a large fore-hall or exercise yard, probably for the cavalry which were stationed there.

Caer Gybi (DE) *Anglesey (Gwynedd), in the north part of Holyhead town, enclosing St Cybi's Church*   This is one of the later forts, built about AD 300, probably as a beach-head fortification for ship-landing, and as a defence against sea raiders. The walls, $5\frac{1}{2}$ ft (1.6 m) thick and faced partly in herring-bone masonry, still remain on three sides, and there were angle towers, the one on the NE still standing, its upper part later rebuilt. The SE tower was rebuilt during the 19th century, and from these two towers, walls probably ran eastwards to the shore, enclosing a quay. No other fort of this type has so far been found in Britain.

Caernarvon (Segontium) (NT under guardianship of DE) *Gwynedd* The fort at Caernarvon follows the standard playing-card plan, a rectangle 550 ft (168 m) by 470 ft (125 m) with rounded corners. The ditch system and original rampart were built in AD 78. Substantial remains of the wall and parts of the gateways still stand, and the layout of some of the buildings within the fort are clearly marked in stone. Stone structures followed the first timber buildings early in the 2nd century and there was extensive rebuilding early in the 3rd. Coins found there suggest that the fort was no longer in use after about AD 380.

Cardiff Castle *South Glamorgan* The fort was built in the 4th century AD with the primary object of defence against Irish raiders. Parts of its walls, which were 10 ft (3 m) thick at the base and had a rampart behind them, have been excavated and reconstructed. It had one gate on each shorter side with projecting towers, and the N gate has been reconstructed on the Roman foundations.

Though this is not strictly a Saxon Shore fort (see page 142, it was built at about the same time for a similar purpose and reconstruction makes it possible to see what the Saxon Shore forts were like. It was abandoned some time after AD 350 and on the NW quarter of the site a medieval castle was later erected.

Coelbren *West Glamorgan, 1 mile (1.6 km) SE of Coelbren village* The ramparts of this $5\frac{1}{2}$-acre (2.2 ha) fort which linked the fort at Neath (now not to be seen) with the larger fort at Brecon Gaer are still visible. It was built soon after the Roman conquest and abandoned about a century later, the internal buildings never having been reconstructed in stone.

Gelligaer *Mid-Glamorgan, ½ mile (0.8 km) N of Gelligaer* Two forts were built here, the first about AD 75 in timber covering 5 acres (2 ha), the second, about 60 yd (55 m) N of this, during the reign of Trajan. It was the only fort in S Wales to be built in stone from the outset. Enclosing 3½ acres (1.4 ha), it had four double gates, angle towers and the usual internal buildings. Outside was a gravelled parade ground and an entrenched annexe on its SE side containing a bath-house. It was abandoned at the end of the 2nd century.

Goldsborough Signal Station *North Yorkshire, between Goldsborough and Kettleness* This is the best preserved of all the Roman signal stations on the Yorkshire coast, of which five have been identified. A square tower stands in a fort of rather more than 2 acres (0.8 ha), with 4-ft (1.2-m) thick walls, rounded angles, bastions for artillery and an in-turned entrance on the S side. In the 5th century it was overwhelmed and destroyed by fire. Two human skeletons were found in the ruins of the tower.

Hardknott (Mediobogdum) (DE) *Cumbria, 9 miles (14 km) NE of Ravenglass* Of all the forts S of Hadrian's Wall this is the best preserved. It stands 800 ft (244 m) above sea level on a spur of high ground N of the road through Hardknott and Wrynose passes from Boot to Ambleside. It covers 3 acres (1.2 ha) and has a fine view down Eskdale to the coast and across to the Scafells. Square in shape with rounded angles, it was built in stone by Trajan to control the approaches to the pass. It was defended by a stout wall with four gates, angle towers and stretches of rock-cut ditch on the NE, its most vulnerable side. All the four gates except that on the NW were double-portalled.

The headquarters, the commander's house and the granaries have already been excavated, and traces of the barrack-blocks have been found. Some 70 yd (64 m) below the S gate was the bath-house, remains of the rooms of which are now labelled. On a 3-acre (1.2-ha) levelled area to the NE, once locally known as the 'bowling-green' was the parade ground. A good overall view of the fort may be obtained from the fellside overlooking it, or from the summit of the pass.

Maiden Castle *Stainmore, Cumbria* An important Roman road ran from Catterick Bridge through Bowes and Brough, connecting the Vale of York with the Lake District and the western end of Hadrian's Wall. On this road were several fortlets, of which Maiden Castle, guarding the Stainmore Pass, was one of the most important. The fortlet was only $\frac{1}{4}$ acre (0.1 ha) in extent and the 6-ft (1.8-m) thick stone wall still survives.

Hardknott Pass and remains of Roman fort, Cumbria

Martinhoe *Devon, 3 miles (4.8 km) W of Lynton, on the coast*　This was an early fortified post and signal station constructed about AD 50–60. It had an inner enclosure with a gate on the seaward side and an outer one with a gate on the landward side. It could accommodate a century (about 80) troops. After the building of Caerleon on the S coast of Wales, Martinhoe was abandoned (about AD 75).

Old Burrow *Devon, 2½ miles (4 km) E of Countisbury*　This fortlet had an entrance to the inner enclosure on the seaward side and one to the outer enclosure on the landward side. Built before Martinhoe, it had probably already been abandoned when the latter was built. Its earthworks are still visible.

Piercebridge (Magis) *Co. Durham*　This important fort, part of the complex Roman defence system based on York, was built at the place where the Roman road to the Wall crosses the Tees, probably on the site of earlier forts. The need to house large forces of mobile cavalry here was probably responsible for the large area of 10½ acres (4.2 ha) enclosed. Around the fort a large civilian settlement grew up. Part of the fort has been excavated and the NW angle is open to view.

Ribchester (Bremetennacum) *Lancashire, in Ribchester village*　The church, museum and rectory are on the site. The fort occupying 5 acres (2.2 ha), built in the 1st century, stood in a gap of the Pennines, on the Ribble, and controlled this part of the road which ran from the legionary fortress of Chester to Carlisle. Its importance increased with the establishment of the frontier by the building of Hadrian's Wall. It was rebuilt in stone in the reign of Trajan (AD 98–117) and again in 197. The Ribble now cuts through the original site. Only part of the N wall, the N gate and the front ends of two granaries are now visible but the museum on the site contains many finds from excavations.

Scarborough fort and signal station (DE) *North Yorkshire* Visitors to Scarborough Castle will not be able to see any trace of the Iron Age settlement that once existed here, but on the cliff top within the outer defences are the remains of the Roman signal station —a courtyard surrounded by a stone wall, and a square signal tower. It was defended by a ditch separated from the wall by a berm. Like Goldsborough, it fell to Saxon invaders probably in the early 5th century.

Walls Castle (Glannaventa) *Cumbria, SW of Ravenglass* Little can now be seen of this once important 4-acre (1.6-ha) fort which commanded the harbour and the mouth of the Esk. All that remains is the bathhouse locally called Walls Castle. The walls are nearly 13 ft (4 m) high; there are two doorways and parts of five windows remaining.

ROMAN FORTS OF THE SAXON SHORE

Towards the end of the 3rd century AD the eastern coasts of Britain were repeatedly attacked by raiders from beyond the North Sea and the Romans erected nine strongholds to act as bases for dealing with them. They were all on or near the coast, adjoining harbours, had accommodation for substantial forces and were strongly fortified. Seven of the nine contain some visible remains.

The most northerly, **Brancaster (Branodunum)** in Norfolk, now more than a mile (1.6 km) inland, has nothing to show. Of the 5-acre (2-ha) fort of **Burgh Castle (Gariannorum) (DE)** in Norfolk, three sides of the wall and the bastions remain. The Roman walls were later used to enclose the bailey of a Norman castle.

Bradwell (Othona) in Essex has been half submerged by the sea, but part of its west wall still survives, and materials from the fort were used to build the Saxon church of St Peters-on-the-Wall which stands within the enclosed area.

Reculver (Regulbium) (DE) in Kent has also been half eroded by the sea and there is little to see of the remains of the fort.

Richborough (Rutupiae) (DE) in Kent, is probably the most rewarding of all. On the spot where the Roman army probably landed in AD 43 a fine marble monument was erected to commemorate the conquest of Britain. Later this was converted into a lookout post and the foundations still remain. The ramparts thrown up by Aulus Plautus, general of the invading army, still surround it. Outside them are the 3rd-century walls of the Saxon Shore fort and within the enclosed area are the foundations of a pagan temple and what is left of the grave of a Roman officer. The museum on the site houses a great number of relics.

Nothing is visible of the **Dover fort** which is buried under the modern town. The Roman pharos or lighthouse, however, still stands in the courtyard of the medieval castle.

Richborough Roman fort, Kent

Portchester Castle, Hants

Lympne today is no more than a mass of scattered fragments of the walls, which the waterlogged clay soil has been unable to support.

Pevensey (DE) stands on what was a peninsula above the marshes. It is exceptional because, unlike most Roman forts, it is oval in shape. Its 10-ft (3-m) thick walls enclose about 10 acres (4 ha), and its bastions were irregularly placed at positions commanding the best fields of fire.

Portchester (DE) still retains its original almost square shape and 14 of its hollow protecting bastions remain. Roman walls of flint bonded with brick were 10 ft (3 m) thick, and have been refaced in medieval times. To the N of the fort are the remains of the ancient ditch and in its NW corner the Normans built a castle, adapting the fort as a bailey.

ROMAN FRONTIER WORKS

Ardoch *Tayside, immediately N of Braco village*
Ardoch was the chief Antonine fort holding the Tay

valley, and depended on the legionary fortress of Inchtuthil. It practically obliterated an earlier fort which had been occupied from about AD 83, and its five ditches are well preserved on the N and E. The three outer ditches were the first to be dug, and later the area of the fort was reduced by the digging of the three inner ones. All these six ditches are in a good state of preservation. Near the fort were a number of small camps and signal stations but few traces remain.

Bewcastle (Banna) *Cumbria, enclosing most of the village* The fort was built in the reign of Severus (193–211) on the site of an outpost set up by Hadrian to defend the Wall. Unlike most Roman forts, it was planned as an irregular hexagon so as to occupy the whole of the summit of the hill. When excavated in 1937 the site of the headquarters building was found. Bewcastle, however, is more notable for the famous Saxon cross standing in its churchyard.

Birrens (Blatobulgum) *Dumfries and Galloway, 1½ miles (2.4 km) E of Ecclefechan* The original fort here may go back to the time of Hadrian. The visible remains, however, belong to the Antonine fort, 4 acres (1.6 ha) in area. The positions of its stone buildings have been found. The most striking remains today are the large rampart on three sides and the six ditches with traces of an entry on the N.

Burnswark *Dumfries and Galloway, 2½ miles (4 km) N of Ecclefechan* The native fort on this hill, 920 ft (280 m) above sea level, is not easy to see. To the N and S of it were two Roman camps used for siege practice. Of these the S one is the easier to trace, especially the three mounds outside the gates in its N rampart. In the NE corner are the rampart and ditch of a small rectangular fort of late 2nd century AD.

Fendoch *Tayside, 5¼ miles (8.4 km) NE of Crieff* Though nothing remains today of this fort but the site, it was important in its day and deserves a note. Built by Agricola, it was set up to defend the valley of the Tay and, like others, was abandoned after a few years. The site, defended by a single ditch, has been excavated and the situation of its wooden buildings is known.

High Rochester (Brementium) *Northumberland, ¾ mile (1.2 km) N of Rochester* Founded by Agricola, rebuilt in stone by Lollius Orbicus (c AD 139–143), reconstructed under Severus (AD 193–211) and again by Constantius (AD 337–350), this was an important and heavily fortified post commanding Dere Street, the road N into the Forth Valley, and stood between the two Roman walls. It remained after the Antonine Wall had been abandoned. In the 3rd century it was defended by multiple ditches and had artillery platforms on the N and W sides with machines capable of throwing stones of 100 lb (45 kg) to 175 lb (79 kg) in weight to reach Dere Street and the adjacent valley on the W.

Some 4th-century remains may still be seen, including the tower between the S gate and the SW angle, parts of the N and S gates, the ditches on the NE and the foundations of three walls on the NW.

Lyne *Borders, 4 miles (6.4 km) W of Peebles* The fort was built after the revolt of the Brigantes in AD 155 to strengthen the Roman hold on the district. The remains are well preserved and the turf ramparts may be seen on three sides and part of the fourth.

Risingham (Habitancum) *Northumberland, S of W Woodburn, 7 miles (11.2 km) SE of High Rochester, on Dere Street* Like High Rochester, Risingham was one of the outposts of Hadrian's Wall defending its eastern end. Enclosing 4 acres (1.6 ha), it was first built at the same time as the Antonine Wall, rebuilt in AD 205–208 and again in the 4th century. Traces of its ditch system can be seen on the S and W.

South Shields *Tyne and Wear* This fort is most closely associated with the Emperor Severus who transformed the earlier fort here to a supply base for Hadrian's Wall and for the whole land and naval forces in northern Britain. It stood on a prominent hill, now called the Lawe, overlooking the Tyne where the Roman Remains Park is now situated. The specialized nature of the original Hadrianic fort in later times necessitated the building of an extra granary in the Antonine period and seven more in the reign of Severus. The remains of the headquarters building, the W gate and several granaries are open to inspection.

ROMAN LEGIONARY FORTRESSES

The Roman 'camps' or fortified posts, from the legionary fortress down to the fortlet or signal station were all designed on very much the same lines, the smaller ones being simple, the larger ones more elaborate according to the requirements and the number of men to be accommodated. A glance at the chief features of the largest type, the legionary fortress, gives us an idea of what to look for in all.

The shape was usually rectangular with straight sides and rounded corners, the gates being in the middle of the shorter sides and rather towards one end of the longer ones. The commanding officer's quarters were in the centre facing one of the gates in a shorter side. In front of it was the main street leading to the two side gates in the longer side. From the rear of the commander's quarters ran another street to the back gate.

The buildings near the centre of the fort were the administrative buildings and the larger forts had the officers' houses, barrack blocks, granaries, stores, hospital, drill hall and workshops. Each fort was usually defended by ditch and rampart with extra defences outside the gates.

Caerleon Roman amphitheatre, Gwent

There were cases in which the character of the terrain or other special needs dictated alterations in this general plan as to shape, number of gates, disposition of buildings etc., but such deviations did not represent changes from the norm, but only variations in the accepted design.

Caerleon (Isca) (DE) *Gwent* In AD 75 the power of the Silures of S Wales was broken by the Roman commander Julius Frontinus, and the Second Legion was moved from Gloucester (Glevum) to a new site. Caerleon was the point from which the military roads diverged, and its commander was responsible for order throughout all S Wales.

Caerleon, a fort of 50 acres (20.2 ha) conforms to the standard type. In the centre were the headquarters, two rows of administrative buildings, the four streets and the gates. In the W angle were the barrack blocks arranged in pairs, with the centurions' quarters at the end of each block. Excavations since 1964 have revealed the existence of a hospital and a bath-house.

Outside the fort on the W are the remains of the amphitheatre, used for sport and military exercises. It is one of the best preserved in the country.

The fortress was originally of earth and timber. Construction in stone was started at about AD 100.

Chester (Deva)   It is possible that the Roman governor Paulinus set up the fortifications here as a base for the expedition against Anglesey in AD 59. The legionary fortress was probably begun about AD 70 and completed by Agricola at or before 79. It was situated on a sandstone plateau at a point where the Dee, then wider than it is today, protected it on the S and W. Shortly after AD 100 the fortress, enclosing about 56 acres (22.6 ha), was remodelled, a stone wall was added to the earth rampart and the original timber buildings within the fortifications were rebuilt with stone foundations. The northern wall was rebuilt in about the year 300.

In plan the fortress closely resembled Caerleon (see page 148). Excavation has revealed the positions of the headquarters, barracks, granaries, towers and ramparts. Northgate Street and Bridge Street follow the approximate line of the ways to the N and S gates, while Watergate Street and Eastgate Street connect the other two gates, and run directly in front of the site of the headquarters. Compared with Caerleon, there is little to be seen today. At the S end of Newgate Street are the foundations of an angle of the fortress wall and tower. Other foundations are at the Kaleyards E of the Cathedral, and more remains of the N wall are near the Phoenix Tower, best seen from George Street. In Goss Street is the base of a column, part of a colonnade of the headquarters building and in Edgar's Field across the bridge a shrine to the goddess Minerva.

Inchtuthil   *Tayside, 2½ miles (4 km) E of Caputh*
After the battle of Mons Graupius in AD 84 Agricola

149

fully intended to establish the Roman frontier along the edge of the highlands, and Inchtuthil was a key position commanding a long river valley on which forces could quickly be sent in case of sudden attack from the NW, to guard the mouths of the highland glens. His recall and the withdrawal of the Second Legion from Britain made it impossible to hold this long defence line, and all the forts were abandoned. Inchtuthil was deliberately dismantled but, unlike other fortresses, no town has grown on the site and the whole plan can be traced. The fortifications enclosed some 53 acres (21.4 ha). There are visible remains of the rampart and ditch on the E and S sides, the rampart on the W side, the rampart and ditch on the N and W sides of the stores compound and an earthwork SW of the fortress.

York (Eburacum or Eboracum)

The conquest of northern Britain (after AD 70) was accomplished with York as a base. Its geographical position on the main line of communication to the Wall and the northern forts made it one of the most, if not *the* most important civil and military settlement in Britain.

Its existence depended on the legionary fort founded in AD 71–2 and comparable in size to Chester and Inchtuthil, 50 acres (20.2 ha). Like Chester, three of its streets, High Petergate, Petergate and Stonegate, follow the approximate lines of streets within the fortress, and the Minster stands on part of what was once the headquarters building.

Among the main visible remains are the Aldwark Tower, an internal rectangular tower at the eastern corner of the fortress with the wall 16 ft (4.8 m) high fronting it. The Roman wall between this tower and Monk Bar is overlaid by the medieval wall. A few feet of the wall may be seen in St Leonard's Place.

At the SW corner of the fortress is the Multangular Tower, still standing 19 ft (5.8 m) high and topped with medieval structure. Here a stretch of curtain wall 17 ft (5.2 m) high adjoins the tower and there are traces of an internal tower. Later building has obliterated most of the Roman structures within the fort.

In the cellars of the Mail Coach Inn, Sampson Square, is part of a 4th-century bath-house; under the Treasurer's House is the base of a column, and another has recently been excavated under the Minster.

ROMAN ROADS

The Romans were the first people to make roads as distinguished from mere tracks in Britain. These were constructed methodically on solid foundations out of whatever materials were available in the various localities. Long stretches have remained up to the present day, still in use for traffic and recognizable. Even where the original constructions have disappeared, many modern primary roads follow the routes laid out by Roman engineers. In other places these roads may be followed along bridle paths or on parish boundaries and many, unknown before, have been discovered by aerial photography.

Ackling Dyke *Dorset, from Old Sarum (Wiltshire) to Badbury Rings* The A354 follows this road as far as Woodgates when the Roman road goes off in a SSW direction, passing the barrow cemeteries of Oakley Down and Wyke Down, and cutting across the Dorset Cursus. This part, nearly 10 miles (16 km) long, can be followed on foot as far south as Badbury Rings.

Blackpool Bridge *Gloucestershire, off the B4431 near Parkend* This road, which ran from Ariconium (Weston-under-Penyard) to Caerwent, connected the Forest of Dean iron workings with the coast. At this point it appears as a paved trackway with kerbstones along its verge, and the marks of wheels are visible.

Roman road north of Richmond, North Yorkshire

Blackstone Edge *West Yorkshire* The road may be clearly seen mounting a slope to the S side of the A58 about half-way between Littleborough and Ripponden. Towards the top of the hill the paving blocks are exposed and are set, as at Blackpool Bridge, between kerbstones. Down the middle of the road runs a specially laid line of large stones deeply grooved by the brake-poles of vehicles coming down the road.

Wade's Causeway (Wheeldale Moor) (DE) *North Yorkshire, near Goathland S of Egton, E of the road running across the moor* In Roman times a road led from Malton towards the coast in the neighbourhood of Whitby, passing the sites of the four practice camps at Cawthorn. On Goathland Moor it becomes visible for some ¾ mile (1.2 km), E of the minor road. The surface of the Roman road, of rammed gravel, has disappeared, leaving the large rough stones on which it was laid. There are drainage culverts along its length.

ROMAN TOWNS

The fifteen Roman towns listed in this book, including the five associated with fortified posts (Piercebridge, Corbridge, Caerleon, Chester, York) and London are almost the only ones in which the remains of Roman buildings, monuments etc. still exist. In this respect Great Britain has much less to show than, say, France and Italy. Even in some of those mentioned (Leicester, Silchester, the Caisters, Cirencester, Horncastle) there is not a great deal to be seen on the sites.

Much, however, is to be found in museums, but since the Gazetteer deals mainly with actual sites, some Roman towns, notably Chichester, Canterbury, Exeter, Gloucester, Brough-on-Humber and Old Sarum have been omitted.

Aldborough (Isurium Brigantium) *North Yorkshire* The modern village of Aldborough lies within the southern two-thirds of the Roman town, which was the capital of the Brigantes. Its defences enclosed some 55 acres (22.2 ha). The remains of the wall, built in the second half of the 2nd century, may be seen on its SW side, behind the present museum. This part of the defences, open to the public, contains the foundations of two signal towers and a corner tower. Several pavements have been exposed, five still remaining *in situ* and open to the public. Others are in the Kirkstall Museum, Leeds.

Bath (Aquae Sulis) (DE) *Avon* The name, meaning 'The Waters of Sul Minerva' indicates the nature of Bath as a spa and health resort. The Romans were quick to recognize the qualities of its hot mineral springs, and before AD 100 its Great Baths, the temple to its patron goddess and its hotels were already in being and patronized by the wealthy. Around them a thriving settlement grew up, defended in the 2nd century by a wall and ditch inside which were the richer edifices, and on the approach roads, smaller dwellings.

The Great Bath, one of the few remains still *in situ* may be visited, and some of the sculptures from the adjoining temple may be seen in the Museum, including the face of the Gorgon, a relief which once formed part of a pediment of the temple. In the basement of the Royal Mineral Water Hospital are mosaics which were once part of the Roman bath. Parts of the altar of the temple are to be seen in the museum, and one corner of the altar is built into a buttress of Compton Dando church.

These few remains convey little of the atmosphere of this once famous spa with its luxurious houses and hotels, its clean streets, shady walls and pleasant walks.

Caerleon   see page 148.

Caerwent (Venta Silurum) (DE) *Gwent*   The town, founded soon after the Roman conquest, was primarily a centre of trade and a market town. Roughly rectangular in shape, it had at first earth and timber defences, replaced after AD 200 by a stone wall. The main street of the modern village is on approximately the same ground as the road which ran from the E to the W gate, in front of the basilica, forum and temple. Extensive excavation of the town has given a good idea of life in Roman times, but few of the buildings within the walls can now be seen. The walls themselves, with their bastions, have largely survived, and the S wall is among the best of its kind remaining in Britain.

Caister-by-Yarmouth (DE) *Norfolk, W of Caister-on-Sea*   There was once a Roman port here, dealing in trade with the continent. Part of the town wall, of the S gateway and the foundations of a single building, a hostel for seamen, are the only visible remains.

Caistor-by-Norwich (Venta Icenorum) *Norfolk,*

3 miles (4.8 km) S of Norwich Castle The Iceni were settled in and around this town after the Boudiccan revolt of AD 60. The whole of the interior of the town is now agricultural land except for the SE corner where the Church of St Edmund stands. Only the ditch and rampart surrounding the town are now visible.

Chester see page 149.

Cirencester (Corinium Dobunnorum) *Gloucestershire* The fortified post which preceded the foundation of the town was situated at a key point where the Fosse Way crossed the Churn, a tributary of the upper Thames. Here, within 20 years of the Roman conquest a town had sprung up, and already tribesmen of the Dobunni were populating the settlement which grew near the site of the abandoned fort. Of the Roman town itself little remains apart from the Bull Ring which was once part of the amphitheatre. Sections of the rampart and wall are to be seen NW of the London Road and in nearby streets. There is a good museum.

Roman bath at Bath

Colchester (Camulodunum) (DE) *Essex* One of the earliest Roman towns to be founded in Britain, Colchester has a great deal to show to the visitor.

In days before the Roman conquest, Cunobelinus (Cymbeline) King of the Catuvellauni ruled the whole of SE England from his capital here. It was situated on flat land to the W and NW of the modern town and defended by an elaborate system of earthworks and dykes between 2 and 5 miles (3.2 and 8 km) distant from the town. Traces of these may still be seen and followed with the aid of an Ordnance Survey map.

In AD 43 the Romans founded a town on the hill on which the modern town centre now stands. They erected a great temple there to the God-Emperor Claudius, only for it to be destroyed in AD 60 by the insurgent Iceni under Boudicca. On its ruins a new town was built and made a 'colonia' or place of settlement for retired soldiers.

The walls, which still exist for most of their length, were built in the 3rd century and enclosed 108 acres (43.7 ha). Of the many gateways the Balkerne Gate on the W side may still be seen. The second important survival from Roman times is the podium or platform on which the Temple of Claudius stood. On it the Norman castle was later built. The vaults under the castle, parts of one of the oldest buildings in Britain, are open to the public.

Many discoveries of Roman structures have been made within the town but few may be seen today *in situ*. The Colchester Museum has many relics as well as interesting plans and models.

Corbridge see page 113.

Dorchester (Durnovaria) *Dorset* At a point where the valley of the Frome opened out into a rich and fertile plain the Romans, soon after the conquest, founded the town of Durnovaria. By about AD 75 the neighbouring Iron Age settlement of Maiden Castle had been deserted by its occupants, many of whom moved into the neighbourhood of the new tribal centre. The town, situated at the junction of two main roads linking the Devon–Cornwall peninsula with the rest of Britain, became prosperous, and the countryside around was well populated and studded with villas. The Roman remains lie under the modern town and of their plan we know little. There are ramparts on the W and S sides, now overlooked by modern streets, a fragment of wall at the West Gate, traces of aqueducts or open channels on the NW by which the water of the Frome was brought to the town from a point 9 miles (14.5 km) up river, a Roman town house at Colliton Park, and the amphitheatre the Romans constructed on the site of an earthwork at Maumbury Rings on the S outskirts of the town.

Excavations have proved that this earthwork was originally a neolithic henge monument with a bank and inner ditch and an entrance on the NE. When the Romans turned it into a civilian amphitheatre they lowered the floor by more than 11 ft (3.3 m) and raised the banks to accommodate the spectators. This floor, measuring roughly 200 by 150 ft (61 by 46 m), far too large for the ancient town, was probably a centre of entertainment for the whole district around. When in 1952 Her Majesty the Queen visited Dorchester it was the only structure large enough to contain the assemblage of people gathered there. During the Civil War the earthwork was fortified by the Parliamentarian forces to guard the Weymouth road.

Horncastle, *Lincolnshire* Little can now be seen of this Roman town beyond a few sections of the 3rd- and 4th-century wall which enclosed an almost rectangular 6-acre (2.4-ha) area. In 1850 it was visible on all four sides. Finds in the neighbourhood reveal that it was a busy little market town.

Leicester (Ratae Coritanorum) (DE) The site of Leicester, which was on the Fosse Way within easy reach of Watling Street, was recognized as important soon after the Roman conquest. The town was already well established before AD 100 and became the tribal capital of the Coritani. Little is to be seen today except the so-called Jewry Wall, 24 ft (7.3 m) high, once part of a large public baths, and on the Aylestone Road an earthwork called Raw Dykes which may have been part of a Roman aqueduct.

Lincoln (Lindum Colonia) Like Wroxeter, Lincoln was for a time a legionary fortress, occupied successively by the 9th and 2nd legions. Some time between AD 85 and 96 the town became a colonia or settlement for retired soldiers, and from this its modern name is derived. The fortifications followed the lines of those of the earlier legionary fort enclosing some 42 acres (16.9 ha). Parts of the wall and ditch are still visible at East Bight near the Newport Gate. This gate is one of the best preserved in Britain. Parts of the East Gate have been laid bare and may be seen.

Late in the 2nd century a defensive wall was built to enclose the slope of the hill towards the river, taking in the 56 acres (22.6 ha) of the 'lower town'. Of these fortifications little remains except part of the wall and ditch in Temple Gardens. The remains of buildings and many pavements have been found. Much material is on view in the City Museum.

London see page 122.

Piercebridge see page 141.

St Albans (Verulamium) (DE) *Hertfordshire* The pre-Roman settlement here was at Prae Wood $1\frac{1}{4}$ miles (2 km) W of the town. Little of it is to be seen today.

The first Roman town was on the area N of St Michael's Church between Prae Wood and the River Ver. It was destroyed in the Boudiccan rising and the rebuilding was completed by AD 79. The defences of this period can only be seen on the NW corner of the Roman town. In AD 200 the defences were rebuilt, enclosing 200 acres (81 ha). Among the visible remains are the SW gateway leading to London, part of the town wall and ditch in the SW corner of the ancient town, parts of a house, a mosaic pavement and a hypocaust S of the Museum, and the Roman theatre.

Silchester (Calleva Atrebatum) *Hampshire* Apart from the walls, which still survive, very little of the town can now be seen. In King John's reign (AD 1199–1216) the plan of its streets could probably be made out, but in Leland's time (1691–1766) there was nothing left except parts of the wall. Just outside the NE corner of the town the earthworks of the amphitheatre are now overgrown, but may be traced.

From the point of the archaeologist, however, the site has been most productive, since it was not afterwards built on. The whole plan has therefore been discovered and a great deal of valuable material found. The excavations are now filled in and the area is under the plough.

Roman amphitheatre, St Albans

Wall (Letocetum) (NT under guardianship of DE)
Staffordshire   Wall was an important posting station along Watling Street. Part of its triple-ditch system can be seen from the air as a cropmark in the fields to the S of the main street but these are not visible at ground level. The town, however, contains the most complete Roman bath-house so far found in Britain. In it are the remains of many rooms, a furnace and a very well-preserved hypocaust.

Wroxeter (Viroconium Cornoviorum) (DE) *Salop*
Wroxeter was the Roman capital of the Cornovii tribe. It preceded Chester as a legionary fortress. Its position at a river crossing and guarding a N–S and E–W road junction made it important, the fourth in size of all the Roman towns in Britain. It was rebuilt under Hadrian. Later, after fires in AD 155 and 286 the forum and basilica were twice rebuilt.

The site is now cut in two by a road. Visible remains are the baths and part of the wall enclosing them, with the bases of the pillars of a long colonnade forming the portico of the forum.

The town was in decline in the 4th century and had been abandoned by AD 400.

York   see page 150.

ROMAN VILLAS

Bignor *Sussex, on E side of Bignor village*   Several stages of development were discovered here, starting with a cottage house of five rooms to which a front corridor and side rooms were added. In the 4th century wings were added to enclose a rectangular courtyard with an outer courtyard on the SE side. Six rooms with mosaic floors can be seen and the sites of other rooms are marked out in stone or concrete. There is a small museum on the site.

Heat bath at Chedworth Roman villa, Gloucestershire

Brading *Isle of Wight, on S side of the town* The villa consists of a main building with a corridor and a wing at each end. It was later enlarged by the addition of more rooms at the back including a large dining-room. Many rooms have fine mosaic pavements representing scenes from classical legend. Part of a N wing is still visible though most of it has been covered over. It had a hall and many smaller rooms for staff and servants. There was also a detached S wing containing storehouse and stables. Between the N wing and the main building is an ornamental fountain. A large courtyard was thus enclosed on three of the four sides.

Chedworth (NT under guardianship of DE) *Gloucestershire, 3 miles (4.8 km) NW of Fossbridge* This villa, one of the best preserved in Britain, occupies a fine E-facing site at the head of a secluded valley. It has a completely enclosed courtyard, a N wing at a higher level and there was also once a S wing. A spring at the NW corner supplied water for the bath suite

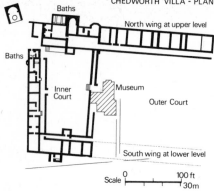

Baths

North wing at upper level

Baths

Inner Court

Museum

Outer Court

South wing at lower level

Scale 0 ___ 100 ft
0 ___ 30 m

which was extended and reconstructed. The hypocaust, the mosaic pavements and the elaborate installations for bathing give some idea of the luxury in which its owners lived.

Fishbourne *Sussex, 1½ miles (2.4 km) W of Chichester*
The villa stood on a site previously occupied by a small Roman military base, set up to overlook Chichester harbour. Late in the 1st century after the army had vacated it, the building of a large villa was begun. It consisted of four ranges of rooms enclosing a very large rectangular area 320 ft by 256 ft (98 m by 78 m). There were two small courtyards in the N wing and on to these a number of rooms opened. The W wing contained a large reception or audience chamber which faced the eastern entrance across the courtyard or garden. There was a bath suite, two more small courtyards, an entrance hall and a large aisled hall in the E wing. Many of the rooms had mosaic pavements. Though nothing is known of the southern range of buildings, everything indicates that this was the home, if not of a royal family, at least of a noble and rich one.

At the end of the 3rd century a fire destroyed the villa leaving only the walls standing.

There is a museum containing photographs, models and relics on the site.

Great Witcombe (DE) *Gloucestershire, 3 miles (4.8 km) SE of Gloucester near crossing of the A46 and A417* The villa, first excavated in 1818, was found to be built on three sides of a courtyard. The hypocaust and mosaic pavements from the bath suite in the W wing date from the 3rd to 4th century and are still on view.

Keynsham Somerdale, *Avon, just W of Keynsham, at the entrance of the factory of J. S. Fry and Sons* Here, just W of the A4 was a 50-room Roman villa of which little now remains. To the E was a building and bath suite of which the foundations may be seen and which has been reconstructed on a more accessible site.

Kings Weston (DE) *on the N side of Kings Weston Hill, Bristol* Kings Weston is one of the winged corridor type of villas with a front corridor and porch, and back rooms grouped round an area, probably once gravelled. Only the plan of the front has been recovered. Three out of the five rooms of this part of the villa are open and one contains a small museum.

Lullingstone (DE) *Kent, $\frac{1}{2}$ mile (0.8 km) NW of Eynsford Station* Though not all the villa is open to view, what can be seen makes it one of the most spectacular in Britain. It consisted of a group of buildings overlooking the River Darent and was the centre of a large corn-growing estate. In the 1st century AD it consisted of a simple corridor building with side rooms, one of these a kind of cellar, now called the Deep Room. Later a circular temple was built behind the house, a suite of bathing apartments, exterior kitchens and special rooms, including the Deep Room, were reserved for private worship.

After being deserted round about AD 200 for some 50 years, the villa was reoccupied, the kitchen became a tannery, the Deep Room was used for marble portraits and busts, and the large granary was built. In the 4th century a temple-mausoleum was added on a terrace behind the house, mosaic floors were laid and other extensions made. In the last, late 4th-century phase, the villa was owned by a Christian family, and this is the only one in Britain in which a number of Christian remains have been found. The greater part of the building is now under cover and open to the public.

North Leigh *Oxfordshire, 4¼ miles (6.8 km) SE of Charlbury* The main house was ranged round a large court, the rooms opening on to a corridor. It probably developed in stages from the small house at the NW side of the court where the residential buildings of the owners stood, with the bath suite. Servants' quarters

'Europa' mosaic, Lullingstone Roman villa, Kent

were on the SW and traces of extensive buildings were found on this side. The villa was occupied until about AD 400.

Woodchester *Gloucestershire, on N side of village*
The villa, probably once one of the most splendid in Britain, had rooms ranged round two courtyards. The great dining-room floor had a mosaic showing Orpheus, with a fountain probably at its centre. The mosaics are periodically uncovered for exhibition. Much of the villa still awaits investigation and discovery.

Rothbury cairns and hill-forts *Northumberland*
Within a short distance in the hilly country round Rothbury are various prehistoric monuments. $6\frac{1}{2}$ miles W (10.4 km), south of Holystone village are the **Five Barrows,** a cemetery of cairns which have yielded cremations, inhumations, pottery, bone pins and flint tools.

S of the minor Swindon–Holystone road is **Harehaugh Hill,** an Iron Age camp with earthworks enclosing $3\frac{1}{2}$ acres (1.4 ha) within multiple banks and ditches.

Two and a half miles (4 km) S of Rothbury is **Tosson Burgh,** a small 1-acre (0.4-ha) fort commanding the River Coquet, again with a bank and ditch on the S and E, and on the N there are steep scarped hill-slopes. The entrance is on the S side through staggered earthworks and a hollow way.

One and a half miles (2.4 km) S is **Lordenshaw hill-fort,** again under 1 acre (0.4 ha), with multiple banks and ditches and entrances E and W through narrow passageways. Inside the fort area are many hut circles. There are groups of cup-marked stones SW of the centre of the fort and on the NE slope of the hill, a group of six cairns.

St Catherine's Hill Iron Age hill-fort *Hampshire, 1¼ miles (2 km) S of Winchester*   On this hill a medieval chapel was built and dedicated to St Catherine, hence the name. The earthworks, a bank, ditch and counter-scarp bank enclosing 23 acres (9.3 ha), were first erected in the 3rd century BC. They were repaired and made higher in the 2nd century, and in the middle of the first, the fort was sacked, presumably by Belgic tribes. After that it was left deserted. The entrance gap to the NE was in-turned and set at an angle from the way over the ditch outside it. During reconstruction it was narrowed and walled.

St Lythan's neolithic burial chamber *S Glamorgan, ¾ mile (1.2 km) W of the village*   The chamber and capstone are now all that remain of the burial chamber, the mound having vanished.

Scorhill Bronze Age stone circle *Devon, 2½ miles (4 km) W of Chagford, just N of the Teign river*   Though many stones of this circle have disappeared, it is still one of the best and most accessible on Dartmoor. Originally there were probably about 70 stones but the number is now reduced to 30, the tallest being about 8 ft (2.4 m) high. They enclose a circle 88 ft (27 m) in diameter.

Snail Down Bronze Age barrow cemetery *Wiltshire, between Everleigh and Tidworth*   These round barrows are arranged in a rough semicircle over ¼ mile (0.4 km) long. They are on Ministry of Defence land and some were destroyed by tank action during the Second World War. Those remaining are of all types. Many have been examined and some have small pits dug into their summits by barrow robbers. One, a disc barrow, has been left open to view. The cemetery was divided from the field systems beyond it by a ditch which ran E to W along the N side of the group, then turned S and continued eastwards along the S side.

St Catherine's Hill, Winchester

Stanton Drew neolithic sacred sites (DE) *Avon,
6 miles (9.7 km) S of Bristol, E of the village* In its
time Stanton Drew must have been as important as
Avebury (Wiltshire) or Knowlton (Dorset) (see pages
71 and 104). It consists of three stone circles, a stone
avenue, a cove and a large stone, once erect but now
fallen, on the N side of the River Chew.

From the first or **Great Circle** of 27 stones (possibly
once 30) the avenue goes NE towards the river,
approaching a small circle, 97 ft (29.6 m) in diameter,
of eight stones, of which four still stand. From this
small circle a stone avenue meets the one from the
Great Circle.

The third circle SE of the Great Circle has 11 stones
and was 147 ft (44.2 m) in diameter.

The Cove is composed of two large uprights and a
fallen stone between them, and lies behind the Druid's
Arms Inn. It is assumed to have had some religious
purpose connected with burials.

The large isolated stone on the other side of the
river, called **Hautville's Quoit**, is the survivor of two.
It stands 7 ft (2.1 m) high and is in line with the SW
circle and the Great Circle.

Stanton Drew stone circle, Somerset

Stanton Moor cairn cemetery *Derbyshire,* $\frac{3}{4}$ *mile (1.2 km) NE of Birchover* Here a Bronze Age tribe had an extensive burial ground and sacred sites. At least 70 cairns may still be seen. A map is essential for identifying the banks, mounds and standing stones. To the N of the group is a circle called the **Nine Ladies** with a single stone, the **King Stone** to the SW of it. To the W, beyond the Stanton–Birchover road is **Doll Tor**, a stone circle of four uprights and two fallen stones, with a ring of smaller horizontal stones at its E end. Cremations, urns and beads were found here.

Stanwick fortifications (DE) *North Yorkshire,* $3\frac{1}{4}$ *miles (5.2 km) SW of Piercebridge* If not the most impressive to view, this fortified area is the largest and greatest engineering feat of the Iron Age tribes. It started as a 17-acre (6.9-ha) fort in the early 1st century AD, and was twice extended until the fortifications enclosed no less than 747 acres (302 ha). It is believed to have been the rallying-point of the Brigantes under their king Venutius who revolted against the Emperor Vespasian in AD 69. His queen, Cartimandua, had taken the side of the Romans and may have set up her headquarters at the fort at Almondbury near Huddersfield.

The first 17 acres (6.9 ha) to be enclosed was a hillock known as **The Tofts**, S of Stanwick Church. Its fortifications, a ditch and bank behind it, are only to be seen on the W side in woodland.

In about AD 50–60 (after the Roman conquest of the S of Britain) another 130 acres (53 ha) to the N of the fort were enclosed by a bank and ditch except on the SE where a stream, the Mary Wild Beck, acted as a barrier. The fortifications between the old and new sections were demolished. Part of this bank and ditch have now been restored.

The final huge extension covering some 600 acres (243 ha) was made to the S of the Beck and brought into the fortified area a rough quadrilateral of land capable of accommodating an army and pasturing horses and cattle. It was enclosed within a bank and ditch with an in-turned entrance on the S. There are signs that the fortifications were attacked by the Roman commander Cerialis before this section was completed. Part of the ramparts then appear to have been deliberately destroyed. No account of this campaign has ever been found, but the fall of Stanwick opened the way to the N for the Roman armies.

STONEHENGE AND ITS NEIGHBOURHOOD
Wiltshire

For many thousands of years Salisbury Plain was a centre of prehistoric man's religious life. Today the region is dominated by Stonehenge, which is unique in Europe and which for centuries has attracted curious visitors. It is, however, only a part, though the most substantial and best preserved part of this huge religious complex. We cannot therefore consider it without the earlier sites at Woodhenge and Durrington Walls or the neighbouring barrow groups of Normanton Down and Winterbourne Stoke, not to mention the many smaller groups and isolated barrows.

Durrington Walls *2 miles (3.6 km) N of Amesbury on the A345* is the largest sacred site so far found in Britain. It has a diameter of about 1640 ft (500 m) compared with Avebury's 1400 ft (426 m). Unfortunately there is now little to be seen. It may have preceded Stonehenge as a sacred site.

Normanton Down barrow cemetery *½ mile (0.8 km) S of Stonehenge* is made up of barrows of every kind including two neolithic long barrows (one ploughed over) and lies in a rough line W to E about ¾ mile (1.2 km) long. It is the finest group of its kind in Britain. Mention can only be made of the **Bush Barrow** standing about ¼ mile (0.4 km) SE of the piece of woodland. It is the most famous round barrow in England of the bowl type which, when excavated in 1808 disclosed the inhumed remains of a chieftain with an imposing array of goods—a lozenge-shaped gold plate, a belt with gold fastenings, a gold inlaid dagger, a bronze axe, a mace and the remains of a shield. Some of the barrows have been disturbed, others are well preserved and various articles have been found in many of them.

Stonehenge, Wiltshire

Stonehenge from the air

Stonehenge (DE) *2 miles (3.2 km) W of Amesbury, in the angle between the A303 to Wincanton and the A344 to Warminster* This has long been one of the most famous and most perplexing sites in the whole country. An aerial photograph shows clearly the low bank and ditch which lies about 100 ft (30.5 m) outside the stones. On the NE side is an entrance gap from which the **Avenue** runs, crossing the A344. On the S side of the road, in the Avenue, stands the **Heel Stone.**

Passing along the Avenue from the Heel Stone one crosses the ditch, leaving on the left the **Slaughter Stone.** Just inside the bank is a circle of 56 holes, now filled up, called after their discoverer John Aubrey (1626–97) the **Aubrey Holes.**

The main construction was made up originally of two rings of huge sarsens capped by lintels. The outer ring had 30 of these with 30 lintels; the inner ring was in the shape of a horseshoe of five sarsen trilithons. All these had been shaped and the lintels fitted with holes and tenons in the uprights, all the lintels being curved to perfect the circle.

Inside the sarsen circle once stood another made up of about 60 'blue stones'. Some of these sarsens and blue stones remain in their original positions; others lie scattered over the area of the circle.

Excavation has revealed the history of this famous monument. First came the bank and ditch, the Heel Stone and the Aubrey Holes which may have been ritual or burial sites. Then came the Avenue and the beginning of the erection of blue stones (c 2000 BC). About 1800 BC the great sarsen blocks were erected and the blue stones put up in their final positions. This completed the monument. (See Front Endpaper.)

Winterbourne Stoke Crossroads barrow cemetery *1½ miles (2.4 km) W of Stonehenge where the A303 and A360 meet* Like Normanton Down, this cemetery has one long barrow and round barrows of all types. They lie in two parallel lines running NE to SW, the long barrow being on the NE angle of the crossroads.

Woodhenge (DE) *1 mile (1.6 km) N of Amersham, just S of Durrington Walls* Not many neolithic wooden buildings have been traced in Britain, and the existence of this was unsuspected until revealed by aerial photography in 1925. Since then a system of concentric rings of post-holes has been discovered, and these are now marked by concrete pillars. They were encircled by a ditch. The posts may have supported some kind of building, possibly open to the sky at the centre of the circle. In any case the structure was almost certainly used for ritual purposes and may have been associated with Durrington Walls. Neolithic and Bronze Age pottery was found here, and near the centre, the grave of a tiny child.

Stoney Littleton neolithic chambered long barrow (DE) *Avon, 3 miles (4.8 km) NE of Radstock* Restored in 1858, Stoney Littleton is a good example of a neolithic long barrow, with a deep forecourt, a walled passage with three pairs of side-chambers and an end-chamber.

Sutton Walls Iron Age hill-fort *Hereford and*

Worcester, 4 miles (6.4 km) N of Hereford, N of Sutton St Michael   The steep sides of the hill on which the fort stands were strengthened by a massive wall and ditch, with entrances at the E and W ends. The site was occupied in the 1st century BC before the fort was built. The fortifications, erected towards the end of that century, were strengthened before the Roman conquest. Then, some time after AD 43, the fort was taken by the Romans and the bodies of slaughtered victims were thrown into the ditch, where 24 skeletons have been found. Though the site was still occupied, the fortifications were probably destroyed.

Thornborough, Hutton Moor and Cana sacred sites *North Yorkshire*   Thornborough, between West Tanfield and Nosterfield, has three Bronze Age henges, all nearly circular in a line NW to SE. They are of about equal size, 800 ft (244 m), all with small banks and ditches inside and outside, the outside ditches now filled up through ploughing. The northern circle is covered by trees. From the central circle ran a cursus in a SW direction, but this can normally only be seen from the air.

Hutton Moor and Cana circles, 3¼ miles (5.2 km) E of Ripon belong to the same group of religious sites, but have been badly damaged by the plough. Many round barrows and traces of barrows have been found in the vicinity.

Tinkinswood neolithic chambered long barrow (DE) *S Glamorgan, ½ mile (0.8 km) S of St Nicholas*   This is one of the most notable burial places in S Wales. The mound, once rectangular, is now wedge-shaped and has drystone walls round it and lining the funnel-shaped forecourt, from which a single chamber was entered directly with no passage. A large stone blocks the entrance, and over the chamber lies a gigantic capstone weighing about 40 tons (40,600 kg).

173

Traprain Law hill-fort *Lothian, 4 miles (6.4 km) E of Haddington* One of the most important hill-forts in SE Scotland, Traprain Law was the capital of the Votadini. It stands on an isolated ridge which was settled during the late Bronze Age. The fort was constructed in the early centuries AD, at the time when the Votadini were entrusted by the Romans with the protection of the Lowlands.

There is a rampart at the base of the hill to the N which, with other defences, encloses 40 acres (16 ha). Higher up the hill on the N side is a massive stone wall cutting off 30 acres (12 ha). Hundreds of 'finds' have been made here including weapons and tools of the Bronze and Iron Ages, Roman silver plate and coins. The fort was still flourishing in the 4th century AD.

Trethevy Quoit neolithic chambered tomb *Cornwall, ¾ mile (1.2 km) NE of St Cleer* The burial chamber of Trethevy, the highest in Cornwall, is still intact, containing seven stones and a large capstone. One of the seven stones has fallen; another which divides the interior into two chambers, is broken. The mound, still there in the 19th century, has now disappeared.

Trethevy Quoit, Cornwall

Uffington Castle (top left centre) and White Horse (below left centre), Berkshire

Uffington Castle and White Horse (DE) *Berkshire, 1¾ miles (2.5 km) SW of Kingston Lisle* This Iron Age 8-acre (3.2-ha) fort has a ditch, bank and counterscarp bank with an entrance facing NW, at which point the main bank appears to run outwards to join the counterscarp bank.

More remarkable is the White Horse, ¼ mile (0.4 km) NE of the Castle. It may be the earliest of many chalk-cut figures in Britain, 360 ft (109 m) long and 130 ft (38.6 m) high. It is possible that it was cut as a tribal emblem some time in the 1st century BC.

Warham lowland fort *Norfolk, 2½ miles (4 km) N of Little Walsingham* Warham is the more impressive of the two lowland camps in Norfolk. It was defended by two banks and ditches which in places still stand 9 ft (2.7 km) high. It was probably constructed by the Iceni before the Roman conquest and shows signs of Romano-British occupation.

Wayland's Smithy chambered long barrow (DE) *Berkshire, 1 mile (1.6 km) NE of Ashbury* This neolithic barrow, built on the site of an earlier and simpler burial mound, was originally flanked by two ditches, now filled in. Though of the same type as the Cotswold

175

neolithic tombs it is simpler, having an entrance at the S end protected by large sarsen slabs. Beyond them a passage led into three burial chambers only, one at each side and one at the end. Eight people, one of them a child, had been buried here.

Woden Law Iron Age hill-fort and Roman siege-works *Borders, 4 miles (6.4 km) S of Hownam village*
Situated at a height of nearly 1400 ft (426 m), Woden Law overlooks the valley of the Kale Water. First defended by a stone wall and later by two ramparts with a ditch between them, the fort was in use until the Roman occupation when it was abandoned. The Roman army then used it as a practice-ground for siege tactics, constructing round the more vulnerable sides on S and E three ditches and other works lower down.

The fort was connected with the Roman Dere Street which led to the camps at Pennymuir, $1\frac{1}{2}$ miles (2.4 km) N, Chew Green, High Rochester and Risingham to the S. All these military sites are evidences of the intense activity that went on on the N side of Hadrian's Wall.

Another native fort at **Hownam Rings** $\frac{1}{2}$ mile (0.8 km) E of Hownam village was also evacuated during the Roman occupation.

Wayland's Smithy, Berkshire

WOOLER GROUP OF CAIRNS, SETTLEMENTS AND FORTS *Northumberland*

Including the hill-fort of Wooler, there are no less than two dozen sites within a radius of 7 miles (11.3 km) of the town, including sacred sites, cairns, stone circles, Iron Age enclosures and forts. A few of these are listed below.

Coupland *4½ miles (7.2 km) NW* is a neolithic sacred site, still visible, though damaged by the plough.

Dod Law *2¼ miles (3.6 km) NE* has a double-banked enclosure and a single-banked annexe with a number of cup and ring marked stones.

Fordwood cliff fort *5¼ miles (8.5 km) NW* is protected by a steep hill slope on the S and a bank with strengthening works on NE and SW.

Great Hetha hill-fort *6¾ miles (10 km) W* is a 1¼ acre (0.5 ha) fort with double banks and an in-turned entrance.

Hethpool *6½ miles (10.8 km) W* is an irregular stone circle of eight stones.

Old Bewick cliff fort *6½ miles (10.8 km) SE* has steep slopes on the S, two pairs of banks and ditches elsewhere, and outer earthworks.

Roughting Linn promontory fort *5½ miles (8.8 km) NW* has the largest ring-marked stone in the county, a rock 60 ft by 40 ft (18.2 by 12.2 m) covered with markings.

Weetwood Moor *2 miles (3.2 km) E* has a cairn and several cup and ring marked stones.

West Hill Camp hill-fort *5½ miles (6.5 km) W* has two ramparts enclosing about ¾ acre (0.7 ha), with traces of huts.

Wooler *¾ mile (1.2 km) S* of the town has a promontory fort of 4½ acres (1.8 ha), divided by triple banks and with outer defences of banks and ditches.

Yeavering Bell *4 miles (6.4 km) NNW* is the largest

hill-fort in Northumberland, enclosing $13\frac{1}{2}$ acres (5.5 ha) defended by a stone rampart. Inside are the foundations of circular huts.

Though by no means as spectacular as some sites in southern England this district is worth a visit by the energetic and enthusiastic explorer.

Worlebury Iron Age hill-fort *Avon, just N of Weston-super-Mare* A single rampart and ditch defends this 10-acre (4-ha) fort on the S. On the E side there are multiple defences and natural slopes N and W. At the E end were many storage pits. The discovery of skeletons suggests that the fort was taken by storm either by Romans or by members of another tribe.

The Wrekin hill-fort *Salop, $2\frac{1}{2}$ miles (4 km) SW of Wellington* Probably the capital of the Cornovii tribe, this 7-acre (2.8-ha) Iron Age fort has outer works which enclose an additional $3\frac{1}{2}$ acres (1.4 ha). A rampart with in-turned entrances at E and W defends the main camp while slighter defences strengthen the natural slopes outside the whole area. Traces of postholes, storage pits etc. suggest occupation even before the fortifications were constructed. At the SW end of the fort is a low mound, probably the remains of a Bronze Age barrow.

Yarnbury Castle Iron Age hill-fort *Wiltshire, $2\frac{1}{2}$ miles (4 km) W of Winterbourne Stoke* The salient feature of this spectacular 28-acre (12-ha) fort, apart from its massive double bank and ditches, is the elaborate in-turned entrance, comparable in complexity with those of Maiden Castle, Dorset and Danebury hill-fort, Hampshire (see pages 125 and 102). Inside the enclosed area are traces of an earlier fort, and in favourable light a number of 'Celtic' fields can be seen to the NE.

GLOSSARY

adze a heavy chisel-like tool shaped like a hoe, with its blade at right angles to its shaft, used to trim wooden beams and planks before the plane was invented.

agger the raised foundation on which the surface of a Roman road was laid.

amphitheatre an oval or circular area with raised seats all round it, used by the Romans for games, entertainments and military exercises.

Antonine having to do with the reign of Antoninus Plus, AD 138–161.

bailey the courtyard of a castle or fort.

ballista a military engine for throwing stones or other missiles long distances, used in Roman and medieval times.

barrow a mound raised over a burial (see also pages 39–41).

basilica A Roman public building near the forum, used as a hall of justice and a public meeting place.

bastion a projecting part of a fortification, usually raised in stone and designed to strengthen its defences.

beaker a pottery drinking vessel of various shapes introduced into Britain by a group of Bronze Age people.

Belgae the name of a Celtic tribe who came to Britain between 100 and 50 BC and lived in the south-east of the country.

berm a flat surface or level space separating a bank from a ditch in ancient fortifications.

Brigantes a non-Belgic tribe living in northern Britain (Yorkshire, Durham, Northumberland).

Bronze Age the period in prehistory (roughly

between BC 2000 and BC 500 in Britain) when bronze was the chief metal to be used for weapons and tools (see also pages 44–50).

cairn a mound, usually mainly of stone, set up over a burial.

capstone a large stone used as a roof for a burial chamber.

Catuvellauni The name adopted by a Belgic tribe living in Hertfordshire and having their capital at Wheathampstead and afterwards, by conquest, at Colchester.

causewayed having entrances or causeways across ditches by means of level paths.

Celtic having to do with groups of people speaking similar languages, some of which migrated to Britain during the Iron Age.

'Celtic' fields small regularly shaped, usually rectangular plots of land used for agriculture, and situated near a Bronze Age settlement. The name Celtic was given in error to these plots of land, at a time when it was thought they had been made by Celtic peoples.

chambered of a neolithic tomb or barrow having within it a chamber with small chambers opening out of it.

cist a burial pit or burial chamber sometimes lined with stone and with a capstone over it.

Claudian having to do with the times of the Roman Emperor Claudius (AD 41–74).

cohort a division of the Roman army containing between 300 and 600 men.

colonnade a row of columns usually supporting a roof.

colonia a town set apart for the settlement of veterans of the Roman army who were given land outside its walls.

counterscarp bank a small bank on the outer edge

of a ditch.

courtyard house a house usually made up of an outer wall surrounding an oval or circular space, with rooms set round the courtyard, their rear wall being the outer wall.

cove a small setting of upright stones, usually found in the centre of a stone circle or henge.

crop marks markings on the ground where crops are grown or there is some kind of vegetation. Usually seen only from the air and denoting the places where ancient buildings, mounds, ditches etc. once existed.

cup and ring marked stones rocks marked with cup-shaped hollows and with rings usually associated with them, found mainly on heathland in northern England and Scotland. They are believed to have been cut by Bronze Age peoples, possibly for religious purposes.

cursus a long avenue bounded by banks and ditches, used probably for ceremonial purposes and usually associated with long and round barrows. Examples are in Dorset (see Dorset Cursus), near Stonehenge and at Thornborough in North Yorkshire.

Dobunni a non-Belgic tribe living around the mouth of the Severn.

Durotriges a non-Belgic tribe living in and around Dorset.

earth-house see souterrain.

façade the front or principal face of a Roman building or of a prehistoric barrow.

fogou an underground passage in Cornwall, made and used by Iron Age peoples either for storage or as a refuge.

forecourt (in long barrows) the space in front, between the 'horns' believed to have been used for ritual and ceremonial purposes.

forum a market place in a Roman town, usually sited in front of or in the neighbourhood of the basilica.

gallery grave a neolithic tomb or barrow having within it a long chamber or gallery either divided into smaller chambers or having smaller chambers opening out of it.

grave goods articles of war, ornament or domestic use found in a prehistoric or Roman burial place.

Hadrianic having to do with the reign of Hadrian (AD 117–138).

henge monument an area, roughly oval or circular, often containing one or more stone circles, and possibly groups of standing stones, enclosed by one or more banks and ditches and having entrance gaps or causeways. Henges were sacred sites used by neolithic peoples, probably for ceremonial purposes.

hill-fort a fortified enclosure on a hilltop or ridge made by Iron Age peoples and defended by complicated earthworks.

hypocaust a system of flues running under and in the walls of a Roman house.

Iceni a non-Belgic tribe living in what is now East Anglia.

inhumation the burial of bodies which have not been cremated.

Iron Age the period dating roughly from 500 BC to the Roman period in Britain when the people used iron as their chief metal for the manufacture of weapons and tools.

lynchet a bank of soil on a hillside made by soil which has accumulated at the lower side of a 'Celtic' field.

megalith a stone of great size, once a standing stone or part of a prehistoric burial chamber.

mesolithic   having to do with the Middle Stone Age, the period dating (in Britain) roughly from 10,000 BC to 3500 BC, i.e. the end of the Palaeolithic or Old Stone Age to the beginning of the Neolithic, or New Stone Age (from the Greek *mesos,* middle and *lithos,* stone).

mosaic   a pavement made up of small pieces of stone of various colours arranged to form a design or picture and used mostly in flooring.

neolithic   having to do with the New Stone Age, roughly from 3500 BC to 2000 BC when the main material for making weapons and tools was flint, ground and polished (*neo.* new).

palaeolithic   having to do with the Old Stone Age, dating roughly from 500,000 BC to 10,000 BC. During this period mankind used the simplest of chipped flint weapons and tools and gained a living by hunting, fishing and food gathering (*palaeo,* old).

palisade   a fence of stakes set firmly in the ground to enclose or defend a piece of land.

passage grave   a neolithic barrow or tomb having inside it a passage leading to one or more burial chambers.

pharos   a lighthouse to direct seamen.

portico   a structure made up of a roof supported by columns often at the entrance of a temple or public building.

postern   a smaller entrance often at the side of a large gate.

post-hole   a place where posts have been driven into the ground, often discovered through containing a different kind of earth from that around it.

promontory fort   a fort set up by Iron Age people either on a cliff or headland overlooking water, or on a spit of high land dominating plains or valleys.

quoit   the term used in Cornwall and some other

places in SW England for the remains of a burial chamber consisting of uprights and capstone.

rampart a mound of stone or earth raised around a fortified place to defend it.

revetment a facing of stone, timber or turf laid on a bank or rampart to prevent the earth slipping.

Romano-British having to do with Britons who have come under Roman influence and Roman customs, who use Roman pottery, coins, weapons etc. and have adopted Roman methods of dress and building.

souterrain or earth-house an underground passage or compartment used in northern England and Scotland during the Iron Age as a shelter, refuge or storehouse (from the French *sous,* under and *terre,* earth).

tessellated (of a pavement) set in small squares or blocks of brick, stone etc. which may be in different colours.

timber lacing making ramparts of earth or stone firmer by putting cross timbers through them from back to front.

trilithons two upright stones with a horizontal stone lying on top of them, as at Stonehenge.

Votadini a tribe living in the modern border country in Iron Age and Roman times.

wheelhouse a construction, usually inside a broch, in which partition walls are arranged like the spokes of a wheel round a central open area.

BOOKS WORTH CONSULTING

Information about many good sites not included in this book may be found in the following:

H.M.S.O. *Maps* Ancient Britain (north), Ancient Britain (south), Roman Britain, Map of Historical Monuments and Historic Buildings in the care of the State, List and Map of Historical Monuments open to the Public. H.M.S.O. also publishes books on chosen regions (e.g. Anglesey, Tayside) and on individual sites. Leaflets on many of these are also available. Consult H.M.S.O. lists. See also booklets published by the National Trust and lists of B.B.C. publications (e.g. *Cradle of England* by Barry Cunliffe; *Silbury Hill* by Richard Atkinson).

Illustrated Regional Guides to Ancient Monuments are published by H.M.S.O. in six volumes: Northern England, Southern England, East Anglia and the Midlands, South Wales, North Wales, Scotland.

In addition to prehistoric and Roman sites these books deal with many more recent ones. The books on Wales and Scotland are specially rewarding.

Discovering Regional Archaeology series in 7 books: Central England, Cotswold and the Upper Thames, Eastern England, North-Western England, South-Western England, Wessex, North-Eastern England.

There is an introduction to this series by James Dyer: *Discovering Archaeology in England and Wales*.

These books give accounts of all the important sites and are published by Shire Publications Ltd, Tring, Herts. Detailed directions are given for reaching every site.

James Dyer. *Southern England, an Archaeological Guide* (hardback and paperback). Faber. A most valuable book.

Nicholas Thomas. *A Guide to Prehistoric England*. Batsford. The chief sites in all the English counties are given in this one volume. There is an interesting and concise introduction.

R. G. Collingwood and Ian Richmond. *The Archaeology of Roman Britain*. Methuen. An indispensable book for those wishing to study this period in greater depth.

Ginn and Co. (History Patch Series) publish booklets and slides on Bath, Colchester, Leicester, Chester, York, London, Cirencester and St Albans.

H. E. Priestley, *Britain under the Romans*. Warne. Gives a general picture of social life in Roman Britain and refers to many sites mentioned in this book.

Many local authorities and museums publish handbooks. See Guildhall Museum, *Handbook to Roman London;* Newport Museum, *The Roman Caerwent Collection;* Caermarthen County Museum, *The Roman Gold Mines at Dolaucothi;* Colchester Corporation, *The Story of Roman Colchester;* St Albans City Council, *Verulamium* etc.

Among important archaeological works published by societies are those of the Cheshire Community Council, the Lincolnshire Local History Society, The Dorset Natural History and Archaeological Society and for Scotland, Buteshire Natural History Society and Bute Museum. See also the Dalesman Mini-Book on *Hardknott Castle* by Tom Garlick (Dalesman Publishing Co, Clapham, North Yorkshire) and *Hadrian's Wall, A Practical Guide to the Visible Remains* by R. W. Davies (Sunderland College of Education, Ryhope Road, Sunderland).

INDEX

186

187

188

189

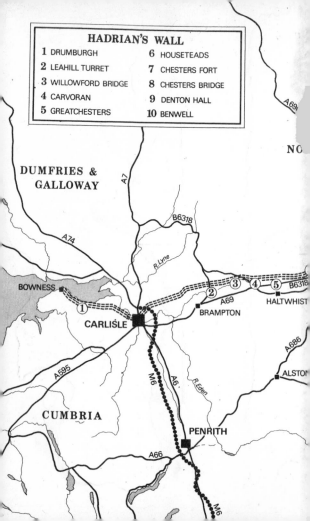

HADRIAN'S WALL

1 DRUMBURGH
2 LEAHILL TURRET
3 WILLOWFORD BRIDGE
4 CARVORAN
5 GREATCHESTERS

6 HOUSESTEADS
7 CHESTERS FORT
8 CHESTERS BRIDGE
9 DENTON HALL
10 BENWELL

DUMFRIES &
GALLOWAY

NO

A7

A74

B6318

R. Lyne

BOWNESS

①

②

③

④

⑤

B6318

HALTWHIST

CARLISLE

A69

BRAMPTON

A595

A686

ALSTON

A6

R. Eden

M6

CUMBRIA

PENRITH

A66

M6